Praise for the work of Alain Mabanckou

Broken Glass

"Whatever else might be in short supply in the Congo depicted by Alain Mabanckou, imagination and wit aren't . . . *Broken Glass* is a whistlestop tour of French literature and civilization, [but while] its cultural and intertextual musings could fuel innumerable doctorates, the real meat of *Broken Glass* is its comic brio, and Mabanckou's jokes work the whole spectrum of humour . . . Much of the writing from Africa (or at least most of the stuff we get to see) is of an earnest or grim character, and it makes a pleasant change to encounter a writer who isn't afraid of a laugh."   —*The Guardian* (U.K.)

"This is not cute Africa, as described by Alexander McCall Smith . . . Mabanckou is one of Africa's liveliest and most original voices, and this novel pulses with energy and invention."   —*The Times* (U.K.)

"A dizzying combination of erudition, bawdy humor and linguistic effervescence."   —*Financial Times*

"Mabanckou . . . positions himself at the margins, tapping the tradition founded by Celine, Genet and other subversive writers. His bursts of grandiloquent magical realism are a promising approach for a region where realism and naturalism have become blunted in the face of intractable problems."   —*The Independent* (U.K.)

"One of the most entertaining reads of the year . . . sad but hilarious raw and gritty stories . . . Great voice; great reading."
                                                       —*The Barcelona Review*

"[Mabanckou's] voice is original and penetrating, his language irreverent and precise . . . His inventive wordplays, his love of books and his desire to break down clichéd perceptions of African and European literatures and cultures create a world in which every reader will find a home. *Broken Glass* is an exuberant comic novel, the perfect antidote for those still looking for Africa's burning libraries."   —*The National*

"Witty, silly, funny and vivid, it is an insouciant novel in the very best sense."   —*Spike Magazine*

African Psycho

"This is *Taxi Driver* for Africa's blank generation . . . a deftly ironic Grand Guignol, a pulp fiction vision of Frantz Fanon's 'wretched of the earth' that somehow manages to be both frightening and self-mocking at the same time."
—*Time Out New York*

"Disturbing—and disturbingly funny."
—*New Yorker*

"Mabanckou manages to write playfully about an alarming subject."
—*Financial Times*

"A macabre but comical take on a would-be serial killer."
—*Vanity Fair*

"The auspicious North American debut from a francophone author who most certainly deserves to be discovered . . . smart, stylish and plenty 'literary' . . . The French have already called [Mabanckou] a young writer to watch. After this debut, I certainly concur."
—*Globe and Mail* (Canada)

"Mabanckou's novel . . . discovers a fascinating new way to hang readers on those tenterhooks . . . *African Psycho* presents no gloomy Raskolnikov, nor the fixed sneer of Patrick Bateman, but a haunted burlesque."
—*The Believer*

"Blackly funny . . . this is a distinctive contribution to the slum-fiction genre."
—*The New Statesman* (U.K.)

"Taut . . . Dark and darkly comic . . . brings into sharp relief the life of an outsider, an anti-hero."
—*The National*

"Alain Mabanckou is like this tree he has evoked in his poetry: Tall, graceful, peaceful, yet a powerhouse of ideas. One of the foremost voices in Francophone literature, this poet-novelist from Congo Brazzaville has always drawn from his African roots."
—*The Hindu* (India)

Alain Mabanckou was born in 1966 in the Congo. He currently lives in California, where he teaches French literature at UCLA. One of Africa's major writers, he is the author of six volumes of poetry and six novels. He received the prestigious Prix Renaudot for *Memoirs of a Porcupine*. He was selected by the French journal *Lire* as one of the fifty writers to watch out for this century.

Also by Alain Mabanckou

African Psycho

BROKEN GLASS

ALAIN MABANCKOU

Translated by Helen Stevenson

Soft Skull Press
New York

First published in the United Kingdom by Serpent's Tail, an imprint of
Profile Books Ltd, 3A Exmouth House, Pine Street, London EC1R 0JH, U.K.

Library of Congress Cataloging-in-Publication Data

Mabanckou, Alain, 1966-
[Verre cassé. English]
Broken glass / Alain Mabanckou ; translated by Helen Stevenson.
p. cm.
ISBN-13: 978-1-59376-273-5
ISBN-10: 1-59376-273-9
1. Alcoholics—Fiction. 2. Bars (Drinking establishments)—
Congo (Democratic Republic)—Fiction. 3. Congo (Democratic
Republic)—Fiction. 4. Self-perception—Fiction. I. Title.

PQ3989.2.M217V4713 2010
843.914—dc22
2009053525

Cover design by Aaron Artessa
Designed and typeset at Neuadd Bwll, Llanwrtyd Wells
Printed in the United States of America

Soft Skull Press
An Imprint of Counterpoint LLC
2117 Fourth Street
Suite D
Berkeley, CA 94710

www.softskull.com
www.counterpointpress.com

Distributed by Publishers Group West

10 9 8 7 6 5 4 3 2 1

To Pauline Kengué, my mother

First Part

let's say the boss of the bar Credit Gone West gave me this notebook to fill, he's convinced that I—Broken Glass—can turn out a book, because one day, for a laugh, I told him about this famous writer who drank like a fish, and had to be picked up off the street when he got drunk, which shows you should never joke with the boss, he takes everything literally, when he gave me this notebook he said from the start it was only for him, no one else would read it, and when I asked why he was so set on this notebook, he said he didn't want Credit Gone West just to vanish one day, and added that people in this country have no sense of the importance of memory, that the day when grandmothers reminisced from their deathbeds was gone now, this is the age of the written word, that's all that's left, the spoken word's just black smoke, wild cat's piss, the boss of Credit Gone West doesn't like ready-made phrases like "*in Africa, when an old person dies, a library burns,*" every time he hears that worn-out cliché he gets mad, he'll say "*depends which old person, don't talk crap, I only trust what's written down,*" so I thought I'd jot a few things down here from time to time, just to make him happy, though I'm not sure what I'm saying, I admit I've begun to quite enjoy it, I won't tell him that, though, he'll get ideas and start to push me to do more and more, and I want to be free to write when I want, when I can, there's nothing worse than forced labor, I'm not his ghost, I'm writing this for myself as well, that's why I wouldn't want to be in his shoes when he reads these pages, I don't intend to spare him or anyone else, by the time he reads this, though, I'll no longer be one of his customers, I'll be dragging my bag of bones about some other place, just slip him the document quietly before I go, saying "mission accomplished"

I'll start by describing the row that broke out when the bar first opened, explain a bit about the sufferings of the boss, some people wanted to see him taking his final breath, drawing up his Judas testament, it began with the church people, who, noticing their Sunday congregations had dwindled, launched a holy war, flinging their Jerusalem Bibles at the door of Credit Gone West, saying if things went on like this it would be the end of Sunday Mass in our district, there'd be no more trances during the singing, no more Holy Spirit descending on Trois-Cents, no more crispy black wafers, no more sweet wine, the blood of Christ, no more choir-boys, no more pious sisters, no more candles, no more alms, no more First Communion, no more Second Communion, no more catechism, no more baptism, no more anything, and everyone would go straight to hell, and after that the Weekend-and-Bank-Holiday-Cuckolds Club waded in, claiming it was largely due to Credit Gone West that their wives no longer cooked for them properly, or respected them as wives did in the old days, they said respect was important, that no one respects a husband like a wife does, that's always been the way of things, ever since Adam and

Eve, and as good family men they saw no reason to change, let their wives continue to grovel and cringe, to follow men's orders, all this they said, but it had no effect, and then we had threats from some old club of ex-alcoholics, who'd gone over to water, Fanta, Pulp'Orange, syrup, Senegalese jungle juice, grapefruit juice, and contraband Cola lite traded for hashish in Nigeria, a righteous band of brothers who set siege to the bar for forty days and forty nights, but again all in vain, and then there was some mystical action from the guardians of traditional moral values, the tribal leaders with their gris-gris, which they flung at the door of the bar, casting curses at the boss of Credit Gone West, summoning up the voices of the dead, bringing forth prophecies, saying the barkeeper would die a slow and painful death, they would nudge him gently toward to his own scaffold, but that didn't work either, and finally there was direct action from a group of thugs who were paid by some old assholes from the district, nostalgic for the days of the Case de Gaulle, for the life of a houseboy, the life of the faithful negro with his service medal, for the days of the Colonial Exhibition and the negro balls, with Josephine Baker leaping about in a skirt made out of bananas, and these paragons of respectability set snares without end for the boss, with their thugs in hoods who came at the dead of night, at the darkest hour, armed with iron bars from Zanzibar, with clubs and cudgels from medieval Christendom, poisoned spears from the time of Chaka Zulu, sickles and hammers from the Communist block, catapults from the Hundred Years' War, Gallic billhooks, pygmy hoes, Molotov cocktails from May '68, machetes left over from a killing spree in Rwanda, slings from the famous fight between David and Goliath, with all this heavy arsenal they came, but again, in vain, though they managed to destroy one part of the bar, and it was the talk of the town, and all over the papers, *La Rue Qui Meurt, La Semaine*

Africaine, Mwinda, Mouyondzi Tribune, tourists even came from neighboring countries to get a close look, like pilgrims at the Wailing Wall, taking masses of photos, like tourists, I don't know what for, but all the same, they took photos, and some of them even came from our own town, people who'd never set foot in Trois-Cents before, and were amazed to discover it, and wondered how on earth people could live quite happily surrounded by rubbish, pools of stagnant water, the carcasses of domestic animals, burned-out vehicles, slime, dung, gaping holes in the roads, houses on the point of collapse, and our bartender gave interviews all over the place, our bartender became a martyr overnight, and our bartender sprang up on every TV channel overnight, and spoke in the Lingala of the north, in the Munukutuba of the people of the Mayombe Forest, in the Bemba of the inhabitants of the bridge of Mouloukoulu, who settle their quarrels with knives, and now everybody knew him, suddenly he was famous, people felt sorry for him, they wanted to help him, and even sent letters of support and petitions on behalf of the good guy they started to call "the Stubborn Snail," but the ones who really backed him were the drunks, who always stay loyal till the last bottle runs dry, and they decided to strike back and rolled up their sleeves to put right the damage caused by the people nostalgic for the days of the Colonial Exhibition, the Case de Gaulle, Josephine Baker's negro balls, and for some this trivial matter became a national issue, they called it "the Credit Gone West Affair," the government discussed it in cabinet, and certain leading politicians called for its immediate and permanent closure, while others opposed such a move, for scarcely more convincing reasons, and the country suddenly found itself divided over this petty spat until, with the authority and wisdom for which he became renowned, the minister for agriculture, commerce, and small and large businesses, Albert

Zou Loukia, raised his voice in a memorable contribution to the debate, a contribution now regarded in these parts as one of the finest political speeches ever made, Minister Zou Loukia spoke, saying several times, "I accuse, I accuse," a remark so stupifyingly brilliant that at the slightest excuse—a minor dispute, or some slight injustice—people in the street started saying "I accuse," and even the head of government told his spokesman that the minister for agriculture was a fine speaker, and that his popular catchphrase "I accuse" would go down in history, and the Prime Minister promised that in the next reshuffle the minister for agriculture would be given the portfolio for Culture, all you had to do was cross out the first four letters of *agriculture*, and to this very day it is widely agreed that the minister's speech was quite brilliant, quoting entire pages from books by the kind of great writers people like to quote at the dinner table, sweating as he always did when he was proud of having seduced an audience with his erudition, and that is how he came to defend Credit Gone West, first praising the initiative of the Stubborn Snail, who he knew very well as they'd been at elementary school together, and then summing up by saying—I quote from memory: *"Ladies and Gentlemen of the Cabinet, I accuse, I wish to distance myself from our current moribund social climate, I refuse to condone this witch hunt by my presence in the government, I accuse the shabby treatment meted out to a man who has done no more than draw up a route map for his own existence, I accuse the cowardly and retrograde machinations we have witnessed in recent times, I accuse the uncivil nature of these barbarous acts, orchestrated by men of bad faith, I accuse the indecency and insubordination which have become common currency in this country, I accuse the sly complicity of all those who arm the thugs, I accuse man's contempt for his fellow man, the want of tolerance, the abandonment of our values, the rising tide of hatred, the inertia of the individual conscience, the slimy toads in our midst and all around us, yes, Ladies and Gentlemen of the Cabinet, just look at how the Trois-Cents has become a sleepless fortress, with a face of stone, while the man we now call the Stubborn Snail, quite apart from the fact that he's an old school friend of mine, and a very intelligent man, this man who today is being hounded is the victim of a cabal, Ladies and Gentlemen of the Cabinet, let us concentrate instead on the pursuit of real criminals, whereby I accuse those who with impunity paralyze the proper function of our institutions, those who openly break the chain of solidarity which we have inherited from our ancestors, the Bantu, I tell you the only crime of the Stubborn Snail is to have shown his fellow countrymen that each one of us, in his own way, can contribute to the transformation of human nature, just as the great Saint Exupéry has shown us in his* work Wind, Sand and Stars *and that is why I accuse, and will go on accusing forever"*

the day after Minister Zou Loukia's speech, the president of the republic himself, Adrien Lokouta Eleki Mingi, flew into a rage, stamping his favorite daily dessert of grapes beneath his feet, and we were informed by Radio-Curbside FM that President Adrien Lokouta Eleki Mingi, who also happened to be General of the Armies, was jealous of the minister of agriculture's phrase— "I accuse," indeed, he wished he had said it himself, and couldn't understand why his own advisers hadn't come up with a similarly short but snappy slogan instead of feeding him turgid set pieces along the lines of "*All things, like the sun, rise on the distant horizon and set each evening over the majestic Congo River*," so President Adrien Lokouta Eleki Mingi, in his vexation, mortification, degradation, humiliation, and frustration, called a meeting of the supposedly devoted bunch of negroes in his cabinet and bid them slave as they'd never slaved before, he was through with turgid set pieces dressed up in so-called lyrical language, and the Negroes in his cabinet leaped to attention and lined up, from the smallest to the tallest, like the Daltons in Lucky Luke, when he's tracking them through the cactus plains of the Wild West, and the negroes all said as one man, "yes sir, Commandant sir," when in fact President Adrien Lokouta Eleki Mingi was a general of the armies, and was longing for civil war to break out between north and south so he could write his war memoirs and give it the modest title *Memoirs of Hadrian*, and the President and General of the Armies called on them to find him a phrase that would be remembered by posterity as Minister Zou Loukia's "I accuse" would be, and the negroes in the presidential cabinet worked all night long, behind closed doors, opening up and looking through—for the first time ever—encyclopedias which stood gathering dust on the presidential bookshelves, they looked in large books with tiny writing, they worked their way back to the dawn of time, back through the age of some guy called Gutenberg, and back through the age of Egyptian hieroglyphics as far back as the writings of some Chinaman who it seems had a lot to say about the art of war and was supposed to have been alive in the days before anyone knew that Christ was going to be born by the power of the Holy Spirit and lay down his life for us sinners, but Adrien's Negroes could find nothing as good as Minister Zou Loukia's "I accuse," so the President and General of the Armies threatened to sack the entire cabinet, unless they found him a phrase for posterity, and said: "Why should I go on paying a bunch of idiots who can't find me a decent enduring and memorable slogan, I'm warning you now, if I don't have my slogan by the time the cock crows tomorrow at dawn, heads will roll like rotten mangoes, that's all you are, the lot of you, rotten mangoes, let me tell you, you can start packing now, go into exile in some Catholic country, take your pick, exile or death, d'you hear me, starting now, no one leaves this palace as of this moment, I'm going to sit in my office and I don't want to pick up even the slightest whiff of coffee, not to mention cigars, Cohibas or Montecristos, there'll be no water, no sandwiches, nothing, zilch, *niente*, it'll be healthy eating all round, till I get my personal slogan, and anyway how did this little nobody of a minister Zou Loukia come up with his "I accuse" that everyone's talking about, eh, the Presidential Security Services tell me people are even calling their babies "I accuse," and what about those young girls on heat getting it tattooed onto their backsides and the clients who, in an ironic twist, demand that the prostitutes have it, you'll appreciate, I think, what a colossal fuck-up this represents, it's not even as if it was rocket science to think up in the first place, a phrase like that, are the minister for agriculture's negroes better that you, eh, do you realize, I wonder, that his negroes don't even have an official car each, they get the ministry bus, they live off pitiful salaries, while you loll about here in the palace, swimming in my pool, drinking my champagne, sitting about watching foreign TV on cable, listening to their lies about me, eating my petit fours, eating my salmon and my caviar, strolling about in my garden, taking your mistresses skiing on my artificial snow slopes, I'm surprised you don't sleep with my twenty wives, I'm beginning to wonder why I even have a cabinet, is that what I pay you for, to sit around here all day doing nothing, eh, why don't I just hire my own stupid dog as head of cabinet, tell me that, you bunch of good-for-nothings," and President Adrien Lokouta Eleki Mingi walked out slamming the door of cabinet behind him, still shouting "you bunch of negroes, things are going to change in this palace, I've had it with fattening up slavering slugs like you, let's start judging by results, to think some of you went to ENA and the *écoles polytechniques*, ENA my ass!"

*

the negroes of the cabinet set about their arduous task with a Chaka Zulu spear and a sword of Damocles dangling over their heads while the palace walls still echoed with the president's final words, and around midnight, since they still hadn't thought of anything—there's plenty of gas in this country, but not many ideas—it naturally occurred to them to phone a well-known member of the Académie Française who was apparently the only black in the history of this august assembly, and everyone applauded this last-minute idea, and everyone said the academician in question would consider it a great honor, so they wrote him a long letter full of smoothly phrased imperfect subjunctives, and even some particularly moving passages composed in classical Alexandrines with identical rhymes, they checked it carefully for punctuation, they didn't want to be sneered at by the academicians, who would take any opportunity to prove their usefulness to the world, beside handing out the Top Prize for Best Novel, and the president's negroes almost came to blows over it, because some of them said there should be a semicolon in place of a comma and others didn't agree and wanted to keep the comma to move the phrase up into fifth gear, and those in the latter camp stuck to their point even though it was contradicted by a certain Adolphe Thomas, in the *Dictionnaire des difficultés de la langue française*, whose view supported that of the first camp, and the second camp refused to yield and the point of all this was to get on the right side of the Black academician who, as they were humbly aware, was one of the first ever doctors of French grammar from the African continent, and everything might have passed off smoothly if Adrien's negroes hadn't then said that the academician would be slow to reply, the spear of Chaka Zulu and the sword of Damocles would come down on them before they received word from the

Coupole, which is the name given to the onion dome beneath which these immortal sages sit listening to the distant babble of the French language and decree absolutely that such and such a text is the degree zero of all writing, but there was another reason why the negroes beat a retreat, one member of the cabinet, who'd come in top in his year at the ENA and owned the complete works of the black academician in question, pointed out that he had already produced a phrase for posterity, "emotion is black as reason is Greek," as an ENA graduate himself he explained to his colleagues that actually the academician couldn't come up with a second slogan because posterity isn't like the court of King Petaud where nobody's boss and anarchy rules, you only get one chance to coin a phrase, otherwise it's all just hollow chatter, much ado about nothing, that's why phrases that go down in history are short, sharp, and to the point, and since such phrases survive through legends, centuries, and millennia, people unfortunately forget who the true authors were, and fail to render unto Caesar what is Caesar's

undaunted, the negroes of the President and General of the Armies came up with something else at the last minute, they decided to put all their ideas and everything they had found into a hat, they said it was called "brainstorming" in the smart colleges some of them had been to in the United States, and each of them wrote down on a piece of paper several phrases that had gone down in the history of this shitty world, and started to go through them, like they do in countries where you have the right to vote, reading each one out in a monotonous voice under the authority of the chief negro, beginning with Louis XIV, who said "I am the State," and the leader of the negroes of the President and General of the Armies said "no, that quote's no good, we're not having that one, it's too self-regarding, it makes us sound like dictators, next!" Lenin said "*Communism is Soviet power plus the electrification of the entire country,*" and the chief black said "no, that's no good, it's disrespectful to the people, especially in a country where they can't even pay their electricity bills, next!" Danton said "*Boldness, and again boldness, and always boldness!*" and the chief negro said "no, no good, too repetitive, besides, people will think we're not bold enough, next!" Georges Clemenceau said "*War is too serious to be left to the generals,*" and the chief negro said "no, no good, the military won't like that, we'll have a coup d'état every five minutes with that one, the president himself is a general of the armies, don't forget, we need to watch our step, next!" Mac-Mahon said "*I am here. I shall remain here,*" and the chief negro said "no, no good, sounds like a man unsure of his charisma clinging to power, next!" Bonaparte said, during the Egyptian campaign, "*Soldiers, from the height of these pyramids, forty centuries look down on you,*" and the chief negro said "no, no good, it makes the soldiers sound uncultured, as though they've never read the works of the great historian Jean Tulard, it's our job to show people soldiers *aren't* idiots, next!" Talleyrand said "*This is the beginning of the end,*" and the chief negro said, "no, no good, they'll think we mean the end of our regime, and we're meant to be in power for life, next!" Martin Luther King said "*I have a dream,*" which irritated the chief negro, he hates any mention of MLK over Malcolm X, his idol, so he said "no, no good, we're fed up with utopias, everyone's always waiting for their own to come true, and I can tell you they'll be waiting a good few hundred years yet for that to happen, next!" Shakespeare said "*To be or not to be, that is the question,*" and the chief negro said "no, no good, we've got past wondering whether we are or whether we aren't, we've already settled that one, we've been in power here for twenty-three years, next!" and the President of Cameroon, Paul Biya, said "Cameroon is Cameroon" and the chief negro said "no, no good, everyone knows Cameroon will always be Cameroon, it's not as though any other country's going to even try to steal its identity or its Lions, who are, in any case, unbeatable, next!" The former Congolese President, Yombi Opangault, said "*A tough life today for a sweet life tomorrow*" and the chief negro said "no, no good, don't take the people of this country for fools, why not a sweet life today and to hell with tomorrow, hmm, besides, the guy who said that lived in the most disgraceful luxury of all time, come on, next!" Karl Marx said "Religion is the opium of the people," and the chief negro said "no, absolutely not, we spend all our time trying to persuade the people that our President and General of the Armies is God's elect, and everyone will get steamed up about religion again, don't you know every single church in this country is subsidized by the president himself, come on then, next!" and President François Mitterand said "*Time will take care of time*," but the chief negro got cross at this, you mustn't mention Mitterand to him, and he said "no, no good, that guy took all the time in the world for himself, he spends his whole life riding roughshod over his friends and his enemies, then bows out to take up his seat at the right hand of God the Father, no way, next!" Frédéric Dard alias San-Antonio said "*Fight your brother when he's shorn*" and the chief negro said "no, no good, too many bald people in this country, especially in the government, we mustn't rub them up the wrong way, I'm bald myself, next!," Cato the Elder said "*delenda Carthago*," and the chief negro said "no, no good, people in the south will think it's some phrase in northern patois and the people in the north will think it's a phrase in southern patois, best to avoid misunderstandings, on we go, next!" Pontius Pilate said "*Ecce homo*" and the chief negro said "no, no good, same applies as to Cato the Elder's flights of fancy, next!" as Jesus was dying on the cross he said *"My God, my God, why have you forsaken me?"* and the chief negro said "no, no good, too pessimistic, too whiny, really, for a guy like Jesus, he could have really fucked things up here below with all the power he had, next!" Blaise Pascal said *"if Cleopatra's nose had been shorter it would have changed the face of the world"* and the chief negro said "no, no good, we're talking politics here, not plastic surgery, move on, next!" and so the president's negroes looked through thousands of quotations and all sorts of other historic sayings and found nothing suitable for the country's most important citizen, because each time the chief negro said "no, no good, move on, next!" and then at five in the morning, before the first cock crowed, one of the advisers who'd been flicking through some black-and-white documentaries at last hit upon a historic phrase

at exactly midday, just as the entire population sat down to a delicious meal of bicycle chicken, the President and General of the Armies took over the radio programs and the only TV channel in the country, it was a solemn occasion, the president stretched taut as the skin of a Bamileke drum, it was hard to choose exactly the right moment for leaving a phrase to posterity, and on that memorable Monday he was dressed in his Sunday best, wearing his heavy gold medals, looking from then on like a patriarch in the autumn of his reign, in fact he was so much dressed in his Sunday best, on that memorable Monday, you'd have thought it was the day of the Feast of the Goat, which we celebrate in memory of his grandmother, clearing his throat to overcome his nerves, he began by criticizing the countries of Europe, who dazzled us with the sun of independence, when in fact we're still dependent on them, since we still have avenues named after General de Gaulle and General Leclerc and President Coti and President Pompidou, but in Europe there are no avenues named after Sese Soto, or Idi Amin Dada, or Jean-Bedel Bokassa or any of the other fine men known personally to him, and valued for their loyalty, humanity, and respect of the rights of man, in that sense we are still dependent—they take our oil but withhold their ideas, they cut down our forests to keep themselves warm in winter, they educate our leaders at ENA and the Polytechnique and turn them into little white negroes, the Banania negroes are back again, we thought they'd disappeared into the bush, but here they are, ready for action, thus spoke our president, his breath short, his fist punching the air, and this speech on the ills of colonialism led him on to a denunciation of the cruelty and challenges of capitalism, he said all that was utopia, and worst of all were the homegrown lackeys of the colonialists, the guys living in our country, who eat with us, dance in our bars, sit next to us on public transportation, work in our fields, our offices, our markets, these double-edged swords who do things with our wives which the memory of my mother who died in the river Tchinouka prohibits me mentioning, these men are actually moles of the imperial forces, and let's just say the President and General of the Armies' anger shot up by ten notches at this point, because he hates those lackeys of imperialism and colonialism, as one might hate chigoes, bugs, fleas, or worms, and the President and General of the Armies said they must be tracked down, these criminals, these puppets, these hypocrites—"Tartuffes," he called them, "Malades Imaginaires," "Misanthropists," and "Paysans Parvenus," he said the proletariat revolution will triumph, the enemy will be crushed, driven back, wherever he may appear, he said God was with us, that our country was eternal, as he was himself, he called for national unity, the end of tribal warfare, he told us we were all descended from a single ancestor, and finally he came to the "The Credit Gone West Affair," which was dividing the country, he praised the Stubborn Snail's initiative, and promised to award him the Legion of Honor, and finished his speech with the words he was determined to leave to posterity—and we knew these were the words because he said them several times over, arms stretched wide as though clasping a sequoia, he said "I have understood you" and his phrase too became famous throughout the land, which is why, for a joke, we common folk often say that "the minister accuses; the president understands" as he had told me himself many years ago, the Stubborn Snail first got the idea for opening a bar when he was in Douala, in the downtown district of New-Bell where he saw The Cathedral, the Cameroonian bar that had never closed its doors since the day it first opened, and the Stubborn Snail turned into a pillar of salt and settled in, ordered a bottle of Flag, a man came up and introduced himself, saying he had been the boss right from the start, they called him Steppenwolf, he said, and according to the Stubborn Snail the guy looked like something on the road to extinction, an Egyptian mummy, nothing mattered but his bar, even brushing his teeth or shaving the cactus stubble on his chin was a waste of time, he chewed kola nut, smoked moldy tobacco, it was as though he moved about on some kind of magic carpet, like you get in fairy tales, so the Stubborn Snail asked him about a thousand and one questions, to which he willingly replied, and the Stubborn Snail realized that the Cameroonian had managed to keep his bar permanently open thanks to a loyal team of staff, rigorous management, and personal commitment, he was there at The Cathedral in person, every morning and evening, and his employees, seeing him turn up regular as clockwork, decided The Cathedral was truly a place of worship, with morning and evening prayers and since, as you might expect, Steppenwolf had his lair just opposite, so you couldn't even mention the devil without seeing the flash of his tail, and slept with one eye open, he could tell you exactly the number of people in the bar, who was drinking, who wasn't, the names of those who were just there chatting and not buying, he knew exactly the number of bottles of wine sold, just by keeping an ear out from his bolt-hole and in the middle of the night he'd wake up and walk across Shit Alley to see off some troublemaker, telling him this was a bar and not a boxing ring for Mohammed Ali fans from Zaire, he drew attention to the customer's charter scratched onto a plank of Gabon wood facing you as you came into the bar, you couldn't fail to see it, which declared, among other things, the customer's rights—to order any drink he chose, without fear of contradiction by the bartender, to keep a half bottle behind the bar for the next day, to receive a free bottle for every ten days uninterrupted presence—as well as his obligations, which included not to fight, to vomit strictly in Shit Alley only and not inside the bar, to acknowledge that he entered the bar of his own free will and not because Steppenwolf forced him, to refrain from insulting the staff and to pay for his drink as soon as it was served

throughout his stay in New-Bell, the boss sat around in this bar, closely observing the behavior of the clients and the staff, chatting with Steppenwolf, who had quickly become a friend, at which point he rushed back home, full of enthusiasm for this unusual enterprise, determined to replicate the New-Bell model, but he needed cash, words won't make a dream come true, the Stubborn

Snail was determined, he emptied his piggy bank, borrowed money wherever he could, everyone laughed at him when he talked about his plan, said it was like trying to find out how to slip through customs with a salmon in your luggage, but he gradually got it off the ground, with four tables and a counter less than two meters long, then eight tables, because a lot of people came, then forty tables and a terrace outside, because people were lining up waiting to be served, it was the talk of the town, news quickly spread by word of mouth, particularly since everyone knew that the Stubborn Snail was always above board, paid his taxes on time without quibbling, paid for his license, for this permit and that permit, had produced all the necessary paperwork, including his baptism certificate, his proof of vaccination against polio, yellow fever, beriberi, sleeping sickness, multiple sclerosis, his license to drive a wheelbarrow and a bicycle, he had been subjected to rigorous inspections not applicable to bars which close at midnight, on Sundays, bank holidays, for the funerals of close friends or relatives, or at the drop of a hat, they had threatened to make him go bust, soon, they said, they'd be calling his bar-that-was The Titanic, they swore he'd be eating boiled potatoes, become a beggar, one of God's bits of wood, sleeping in a barrel, like a certain ancient philosopher, and still the Stubborn Snail stood firm, determined as a chess player, and the years went by in dubious battle, till his envious opponents got bored of nitpicking, he resisted the confederacy of dunces, and the other barkeepers all called him names—witch doctor, Houdini, Al Capone, Angoualima, the twelve-fingered assassin, local Lebanese, wandering Jew, and particularly, capitalist, which you'll understand is a serious insult round here if I tell you it's worse than insulting your mother's cunt, or your sister's cunt, or the cunt of your aunt, maternal or paternal, and it's thanks to the President and General of the Armies that we hate capitalists, you call anyone anything in this country, except a capitalist, it can justify the duty of violence, it can justify a good fistfight between social classes, a deadly settling of scores, because a capitalist in these parts is the devil incarnate, he has a fat belly, he smokes Cuban cigars, he drives round in a Mercedes, he's bald, selfishly rich, is involved in all manner of shady deals, in the exploitation of men by men, women by women, women by men, and men by women, sometimes even the exploitation of men by animals, since plenty of people round here are paid simply to feed, tend, and exercise the capitalists' animals, so they called our bartender a capitalist, but he let it pass, though it was a terrible insult, the Stubborn Snail resisted, he hid in his own snail spit, like a true gastropod and it all blew over, the hurricanes, the tornadoes and the cyclones all subsided, the Stubborn Snail bent but he did not break, which was partly thanks to those of us who supported him from the start, because without us he'd have spent the first few months after the opening of the bar dozing behind the counter, he had no loyal staff at the beginning, so he had to get his dishonest cousins to help him out, and they pilfered his paltry takings at first cock's crow, so he'd wake up in the morning to a half-empty till and a mountain of empty wine bottles polished off by the customers, and he quickly realized he mustn't mix family and business, he'd have to hire some responsible, hard-working people, and he was lucky enough to come across two incorruptible guys, simple, good-hearted men, let's say one of them was called Mompéro, he had been an undertaker, he never cracks a smile unless he absolutely has to, you shouldn't even try to tell him a joke, he thinks laughter's unnatural in the human species, and don't even try asking him for credit "you pay up here and now or I kick you out the door," that's what Mompéro will say, I've never seen him argue a point, and I mean *never*, he's got a face of stone, eyebrows like a circumflex, lips like a sink plunger, muscles like a wrestler, they even say that once when he was really angry, he took a whack at a fruit tree though the fruit tree had done nothing, and every single leaf of this innocent tree just fell to the ground, and they also say that when he's angry, really angry that is, you have to get him to drink two liters of palm oil and a cupful of boa fat, and chew on two kilos of onions, just don't pick a fight with him, that's what everyone says, or you'll come off badly, very badly, and the other bartender, his name's Dengaki, he used to keep goal for the Bembe team, more skillful with a knife than a butcher-turned-serial killer, he can catch a bottle in mid-air, is nice sometimes, but not that nice, sometimes his colleague Mompéro has to put him in his place, and tell him there's no point getting in a tangle with the clients, or taking liberties with them, and whenever there is a problem, Mompéro's the one who flexes his muscles, while Dengaki first plays the diplomat plenipotentiary then threatens to get out the pocketknife hidden in the pocket of his pants, so these two guys have been there since the bar opened, they love their job, no doubt about that, when one works the day shift, the other does the night shift, they take it in turns, sometimes Mompéro works a whole week of days and Dengaki a whole week of nights, they've never disagreed on that front, it's a well-oiled machine that's run for years, so Credit Gone West is open all hours, and people are happy, they don't have to clock watch, they're not worrying about last orders from some bartender eager to get home, a bartender who comes along shouting that they're closing in a few minutes' time, "empty your glasses and get off home you bunch of hopeless drunks, go back to your wives and children and try to get down a good bowl of fish soup to sober yourselves up!"

how could I ever forget the man who'd been turned out of the family home like a mad dog, I got a good laugh out of him a couple of months back, a pathetic guy who now goes round wearing Pampers diapers, like a newborn baby, far be it from me to laugh at his condition but that's the sad truth and I hadn't asked him for anything, all I did was look him in the eye and he said, like it was a declaration of war, "What you looking at me for Broken Glass, you want my photo, or something, leave me alone, go and look at those others down there, chatting in the corner," I kept my cool, kept my serenity, there's no point answering back with no-hopers like him, but I did just say "hey man, I'm just looking at you like I look at anyone," "yeah, but you're looking at me strange, you don't go round looking at people like that," and I said, still keeping calm and cool, "how d'you know I'm looking at you if you're not looking at me" and that seemed to really fix him, he was caught in his own trap there, because he said something like "not gonna speak, not gonna tell you nothing about my life, my life's not up for auction," and from then on I knew he was sunk, I wasn't going to listen to that, there are people like that, there's something they want to spit out, so they get to teasing you, pushing you about so they can convince themselves they had no choice but to talk, I've been analyzing customer psychology at Credit Gone West for years now, I've seen that kind of behavior before, "I'm not asking you to talk, brother, you don't know me, you should ask around, the name's Broken Glass, no one ever saw me ask a man for the user's manual to his life, or to sell me his life at auction" and he wound up by saying "Broken Glass, life is so complicated, it all began the day I came home at five in the morning, I swear, and that day I noticed the lock had been changed, because I couldn't get the key in, so I couldn't get into my own house, which I'd rented myself, even found it myself, put down the deposit, I swear on the life of my mother and my father and my six children, I stumped up twelve months of rent including this one before I moved in a single fork, and I'll tell you this I was the only one with a job, I'm not even going to talk about my wife now, or I'll get mad before I'm started, she's not a wife, she's just a pot of faded flowers, a tree that bears no fruit, she's not a woman, I tell you, she's just a whole sack of problems, and there she was, living as easy as a potato from Bobo Dioulasso, easy as a capitalist, just sat there waiting for me to bring home the readies, there she was hanging about all day long, chatting from morning till night with divorced old bags and widows from Trois-Cents, old witches wrapped in stinking *pagnes*, evil bitches who whiten their skin, shrews who straighten their hair to look like whites, while the whites braid theirs to look like the black women, you see my problem, Broken Glass, there was my wife, hanging out with all these tarts who make out they're going to church when in fact they're off to meet their shitty little lovers, I'm telling you, the amount of casual fornication in the churches down there, they don't even respect the house of God, I don't know where God's got to anyway, He's not in those churches, I tell you, those shrews and viragoes are convinced if God does exist, he forgives everything, whatever the sin, and whoever it is has done some idiot thing forbidden by the Jerusalem Bible, I tell you there's some serious fornicating going on in our local churches, no better place for an orgy, some group sex, no better place than the so-called houses of God that sprout up everywhere, everyone knows, even the government people, some of whom actually finance these holy sex dens, but they're not real churches, they're run by religious nuts with shaved heads who exploit, pervert, rewrite, dishonor, seize hold of, abuse and profane the Jerusalem Bible and organize real-life orgies with the faithful, men and women, yes, not to mention the homos, the pedophiles, the zoophiles, and the lesbians, all going at it between prayers, between two Hail Marys, they do it when they go on pilgrimage too, to the high peaks of Loango, Ndjili, and Diosso, when they're meant to be meditating, away from us sinners here below, we of little faith, we philistines, we lost sheep, Pharisees, you're kidding, they go there for casual fornication, and what I say, loud and clear, is "Come down Moses" they've gone mad, doing this stuff on a pilgrimage to the three mountains, and my wife got caught up in all this shit with their guru, she just worships him to death, I tell you this guru, he's been spawning children all over the place, with young girls who can't even change their own tampon when the Red Sea tide comes sweeping in, I tell you this guru guy, he's got money, lots of it, he could keep this district fed through a whole century of American embargo, it comes from you, this money, and it comes from me, and it comes from every single person in this country, I tell you he's superrich, he's a charlatan, he knows all the high-up guys in the administration, he's got some photo of himself with the prime minister, and one with the President and General of the Armies, with the colonels in our army, and it seems he's also the one who provides half the animals distributed to the poor at the festival of the goat, he has his own TV program every Sunday, looking all serious, talking like a black American preacher, and when he speaks on TV he threatens wrongdoers, tells them they're bound for hellfire and the Last Judgment and the rest, that's how he recruits his followers, that's how he rakes in these massive sums of money, there's a telephone number goes up on the screen while he's talking and he has children sitting round him, dressed in white and singing songs of praise to him instead of to the Lord, and people compete to give more than the next guy because they think the more you give this crook, the closer you get to the gates of paradise, but I don't like the way he looks, this guy, he looks like a statue of a fat, mean little Buddha, vicious even, how can you oppose a crook like him, when the army's supplying him with soldiers for his personal security, eh, even if you want to see him you have to make an appointment weeks in advance, and his secretaries won't let just anyone near him, so you see it's not a simple tale of God the Father, it's business, pure and simple, let's speak plainly here, it's a successful business and another thing, this guy has a whole harem up in the mountains of Loango, Ndjili, and Diosso, and it's one big sex spree up there, everyone's at it, and so my wife abandoned the marital home for a week, and went off up into the mountains, not even sacred mountains, they weren't, though to her they were "mountains of the soul"

the Pampers guy seemed to be struggling for words that day, but all at once he got into his stride and went on with his story, without even checking I was listening: "so you see, Broken Glass, my wife has the nerve to say I'm not allowed out, when I'm telling you, she had no right to tell me what to do, I paid all the bills, but she made all the rules, who ever heard of a thing like that, in this crumbling world, eh, no one, that's who, she thinks she can stop me from spoiling myself a little from time to time, as a man has a right to, with the hot little numbers down in the Rex District, you know what I mean, what was I supposed to do with myself while the guru was giving my wife a going over in the high mountains of Loango, Ndjili, and Diosso, eh, what was I supposed to do, fold my arms and watch from the sidelines, reading my Jerusalem Bible, eh, keep the house nice, eh, make her meals, eh, make me a cuckold, okay, but a posthumous cuckold please, make me a cuckold, but not with the connivance of the church brigade, not with the connivance of people who are meant to be showing us the way to the gates of paradise, you know some days, I wonder if some of my kids, all except the girl who looks like me, aren't the guru's kids, anyway, what am I supposed to do with myself, eh, it's true I love those hot little things down around the Rex District, yeah, I love the taste of young girl, especially from down there, real belles du seigneur, they are, they know how to handle the Ding-an-sich, they're born with it, you'll never know fear and trembling like that in the marital bed, they're amazing, Broken Glass, they're little volcanoes, they promise you the earth and then they give it to you, all gift-wrapped, while the women back home are just one big disappointment, those hot little numbers from the Rex District, wow are they hot, they're like rubber, like elastic, it's sharp, it's sweet, it's frenzied, they whisper in your ear, they're with your erection every fraction of the way, they know just where to touch you to wake the slumbering alternator, they know how to keep you from stalling at the roundabout, how to get your turbine turning, slip through the gears, accelerate, you feel happy, like you got your whole life before you, and you know how it is, Broken Glass, it was my money, I had a right to spend it as I wanted, I reckon, why'd she go breaking my balls like that, eh, I'll tell you something, she was no good at it anyway, my wife, if she had been I'd have stayed at home like the other assholes in the district, but she just lay there, my wife did, staring up at the roof, got no choice but to pick my nails and think about the slender little bodies of the Rex girls, she could at least have tried to fake a bit of pleasure, while I was pumping away on top of her like some mediocre cyclist in the Tour de Trois-Cents, I'll tell you an open secret, while I'm at it, Broken Glass, one day she literally forced me to leave off squirming about on top of her, because she was determined not to miss the last episode of Santa Barbara, well then my engine just cut straight out, no life left in it, batteries flat, nothing working, I mean nothing at all, I was impotent, just watching my tool losing altitude and turning into a poor little flag at half-mast, then finally a tiny little thing no bigger than a premature baby's, by which I mean to say I was seriously disconcerted, discombobulated, disoriented, and derailed, I swear to you, I got dressed in a flash, I was yelling my head off, shouting shit! Shit! Shit! I told her I wasn't going to pay any more bills till she started shifting her ass during sex and what's more I said, she could stop counting on me, I'm no sucker, no asshole, no cretin, I got to protect my pride against those slings and arrows, I think maybe I may have slightly hurt her feelings when I said I got married to a plank of wood, she didn't know the first thing about giving a man pleasure, I said the only thing she knew how to bring off in triumph was the act of procreation, and any wild beast could do that, yep, I said all this while I was getting dressed in a flash, I said it in anger and stormed out of the house, slamming the door, and once I was out I ran like a madman escaping from the asylum while the guard is taking a piss, I jumped into a bush taxi, the driver wanted to talk, I gave him the brushoff, because I couldn't think what we could have to say to each other, and he said he reckoned I was worrying about something, it was plain as the nose on my face, and I said he could spare me his reckonings and zip it, just drive me direct to the Rex District, but he went on chatting away, working me over, trying to find out the reason for my despair, but I wasn't telling him, I said if he didn't shut his foreigner face I'd get out of his old jalopy, and he sighed and said it must be about a woman then, I didn't look like a man who enjoyed a happy home life, and I gave a start like "what d'you know about it then?" and he sniggered, and turned round and said "all the guys looking like you do and asking for the Rex District are either cuckolds or have a wife as stiff as a plank of Gabon wood," and I told him again to shut up, "they sure are hot, those girls around the Rex District," he said, I was angry, I just yelled "leave me alone and drive, man," but he wouldn't stop, the asshole, he just kept right on saying "hey, life is beautiful, man, laugh a little, you'll be flying high in a little while, relax, stay cool, breathe easy" and since I'd stopped talking to him, he added with a laugh, "please yourself man, I was only making conversation, still, it's strange the way clients these days, they got no sense of humor, I'll take you to the Rex District, but you spare me a thought when you're getting it on" and he didn't say one more word, just smiled this sly smile all the rest of the way, till at last we got to the Rex District, I paid the asshole driver, but I threw the notes in through the window at him, and he drove off, giving me the finger, I shouted "imbecile!" he shouted "cuckold!" but I didn't give a fuck, I was in the Rex District, where the girls are so pretty, and available, open to all the usual and some of the less usual propositions, so there I was, in my natural milieu, the school of flesh, district Eros-hima, and all the girls knew me, because I worshipped their bodies, their beauty, and didn't just treat them like tarts, I would do the things with them that you do with any normal woman with an ounce of eroticism in her and not one frozen stiff like mine, and one of them asked me that evening if I'd like a special massage, known as the "master's flesh" and I immediately said yes, because this Haitian friend of mine who lives in Montreal now told me it was great, even if it was twice the usual price, I said yes indeed to the "master's flesh" and I sure did fly, and when I got back home at dawn I found my wife had changed the lock, yeah, that's what I said, Broken Glass, after fourteen and a half years of marriage, and then some, fourteen years of deadly boredom, fourteen years in the wilderness, fourteen years of pretense, sham, and faking it, fourteen years of calvary and the missionary position, she'd gone and changed the locks, now I wasn't going to sleep out in the street just because she'd changed the lock with the help of her brother-in-law, a well-known locksmith, I wasn't going to sleep in the street like a bum, no way, so I knocked on the door, got no answer, I shouted my wife's name so loud I woke the neighbors, she didn't open up, I threatened to kick the door in, I would count up to five, I counted real slow, she never came, so naturally enough, I called the fire brigade, since I didn't want to break down the door of my own house, and when the fire brigade arrived with all their gear, thinking they'd been called out to a real bush fire, I explained my house wasn't on fire, but I needed to find a really good excuse for calling them out, because these guys get really bored when there's no fire locally, they often get fed up doing practice runs, some of them reach retirement without ever having put out so much as the flame of a match, and I lied and said the children were locked in the house and their mother had passed out, and they were a bit disappointed that there was no fire, the firefighters asked why I didn't have the keys to my own home, and I said that I'd gone to work a night shift and I'd left them in the house, so my keys were in the house and not on my person, then one fireman pointed out that I really was a complete idiot, and I told him they were his words not mine and the firefighters charged at the door like a band of madmen all trying to get through the eye of a needle at once, and they broke down the cruddy door after a hell of a struggle, and my wife came bursting out of the bedroom, roaring, with her claws at the ready, and flung herself at me like a tigress protecting her two-day-old babies, tackled me to the floor, she's twice my size, and yours too, Broken Glass, she's a real fury, my wife is, believe me, I shouted for help, the firefighters separated us, asked what was going on with us, I wanted to speak first because I'm the man, but my wife slapped me and told me to shut my filthy womanizing mouth, and she lied and said I should stop hanging out round the marital home because the matrimonial judge for Trois-Cents had ordered me out of it months ago, and the firefighters called me a sad liar and a sad mythomaniac and a sad troublemaker, and just totally sad, and told me to get my ass double quick out of the marital home, "the law is tough but it is the law," that's what they said, and I refused to get out because I didn't see what business the law had being tough with me, so I said anyway, I was the one who paid the bills, I'd bought the TV, and the Duralex plates, and I paid for the food, I paid for the children's school things, and I paid for the water, and I paid for the electricity, and so on and so forth, and at that point they called the police because firefighters don't normally carry handcuffs with them, they always turn up with pipes and stretchers and great big engines that disturb everyone and all because someone, somewhere, has struck a match, and it's not their job to send people to prison, they're supposed to put out fires and resuscitate the half-wits and the suicides and people who've had accidents and pass out, and so the police turned up straight away, because the station's only two hundred meters from the house, the one I've rented with my own money, and, get this, my wife told the police I was a dangerous man, more dangerous even than Angoulima, the well-known serial killer who decapitated his victims and stuck up their heads on poles round the Côte Sauvage, and my wife said I was an ex-convict, and a thief, that I dealt in cannabis and Colombian cocaine, and she said I'd stopped sleeping at home, I never washed, that I beat our children to death, that I'd stopped paying the rent, that she was going to be turned out of the house herself, that I slept with the tarts around the Rex, and that I slept with them without wearing proper condoms that come from Central Europe, because according to her condoms from Nigeria are no good, they've got a hole at the tip, which allows a man to cheat on a woman, taking his pleasure as if he weren't wearing a condom, and the poor woman underneath thinks he is using a condom, when in fact it's just a thing with a hole in the top, you know what I mean, Broken Glass, so my wife said I could well be HIV extra-positive and not know, and it was probably quite far gone, because I was getting weirdly thinner and thinner and I had a face like a fish, and my head now looked like a Hottentot's skull and I had constant diarrhea and I groaned when I pissed, and that I often vomited, and she said I gave away my salary to the girls from the Rex District and I had two mistresses young enough to be my granddaughters or the granddaughters of the firefighters, or of the policemen outside our house, God help us, and that's when the situation began to go downhill, particularly when my wife made out I also did disgusting things to our daughter, Amelie, she called me sorcerer, barbarian, caveman, and worse, she told all the people gathered at our house that I got up every night to lay my hands on our daughter, do disgusting things to her, indecent things, and she claimed that I would give Amelie sleeping pills so she wouldn't realize the disgusting, indecent things I did to her, now you tell me, Broken Glass, can you see me doing that, d'you see me sullying the cloakroom of childhood, do you see me nipping buds, can you see me shooting at a child, its impossible, after all, Amelie's my own daughter, isn't she, and I was so shocked, I didn't even defend myself against her false accusations, and in among all the people in uniform there was a cop of the female persuasion with the muscles of a docker and her hair cut short, like a normal cop, I mean a male policeman, and this cop of the female persuasion pushed me up against the wall and called me a bastard, a pedophile, a sadist, she said she'd crush me under her boot, she'd trample on my corpse, and spit on my grave, I was like a sailor washed up in the tide, I should know there was a punishment for every crime, and this cop of the female persuasion swore she'd get me banged up, she promised to do everything she could to make sure there was no fair trial, she said I didn't deserve the honor of a legal trial, besides which they're a complicated business, and she was the one who put the handcuffs on me and her colleagues all took a kick at me, booting me in the balls, as I lay dying at the intruders' feet, I can show you the scars, marks I bear to this day, and I began to cough up petals of blood, petals of blood the size of potatoes from Bobo-Dioulasso, petals of blood the size of dinosaur turds, and they dragged me to the local police headquarters and when they heard there that I was a pedophile, the other policemen all agreed I should be taken straight to Makala, there to spend the next half of my life, Makala is the place all the criminals in this town dread, and that's where they took me, I swear, Broken Glass, it was a bad situation, you wouldn't think it to see me sitting here now, but I spent over two and a half years in Makala and two and a half years in a prison like that is no joke"

I listened to him in silence, he had tears in his eyes and took a good gulp of his drink before continuing his tale, "two and a half years in Makala, it's an eternity, specially when the other inmates have been told you're in there for doing obscene things to your daughter, when it wasn't even true in my case, simply because I could never bring myself to sully the cloakroom of childhood, nip the buds, shoot at a child, and unhappily for me I went through torture, what I went through in that place was worse than what you get if you go to hell, it was dreadful, intolerable, Broken Glass, I don't know how I survived it, can you imagine, the prison wardens, how could they let the gang leaders in the other cells fuck me from behind like that, giving me what they called "the middle way," I promise you, that's what they did, I was their object, their plaything, their inflatable doll, I let them have their way with this little body you see before you, what could I do, nothing that's what, there were too many of them, all clamoring for a go, and when I cried out, because they came so thick and fast these "middle ways," the wardens in Makala just laughed at me and told me to think of the harm I'd done to Amelie, when it wasn't even true, I could never bring myself to sully the cloakroom of childhood, nip the buds, shoot at a child, and every day they took me up the middle like that, grabbing me from behind, I never got any sleep, there was always some guy behind me, whipping me, calling me filthy tart, a piece of tax-free household waste, a vegetable from Tipotipo Market, a cockroach, jellyfish, moth, rotten fruit of the breadfruit tree, all that and more, and sometimes one of the wardens at

Makala took a personal hand in the negotiation of the middle way, a nervous young man who told me he'd never done that in his life before, not to a man, he was no queer, just wanted to make me pay for the disgusting things I'd done to Amelie, when it wasn't even true, and he was the one who whipped me while he shoved himself up my hinterland like a trucker, I tell you, he was hung like King Kong, so that's what they did to me in Makala, they destroyed me, I can show you my backside, you could make a fist and put it up me, no problem, that's the truth, I never even got a trial, in this shit-hole of a country"

when he'd finished telling me his life story, the guy in Pampers raised his glass and said "ciao" and drank it down, poured another one, and drank that down too, then stood up saying "okay, okay," and then I got a close-up of his backside, bulging with four layers of Pampers, a damp backside, buzzing with flies, and he saw fit to tell me "don't worry about the flies, it's always like that, Broken Glass, flies are my best buddies these days, I don't even bother brushing them away, they always find me again, wherever I go, I get the feeling it's always the same flies following me," and then he nodded a last farewell, and I did the same, and off he went to beg in the nearby streets, while I sat there, staring into the distance, watching him disappear and I thought, one day he'll completely flip his lid, he'll come back here and say "tell me who to kill," not that I would go along with anything like that, not for one moment, I'd never be an accessory to murder, that's a different thing altogether, I don't know how anyone can kill, life is essential, that's what my mother always told me, and even if she's dead now, I'll always stick to that rule of thumb, so if the Pampers guy ever takes it into his head to commit a crime, he'll have carry it out himself

I met the Printer the same way I meet most of the new characters in the bar, they just pop up out of nowhere, suddenly there they are, with tears in their eyes and tremors in their voices, and this one, the Printer I mean, had been looking for me, for a chat, ever since the day he first set foot in Credit Gone West, he really wanted to talk to me, no one else would do, and he kept calling out "I want to talk to you, I want to talk to you, you're the one they call Broken Glass round here, aren't you, I want to talk to you, I've got so much to tell you, let me sit down at your table and order a bottle," I just pretended I had no interest in his story, I'd heard so many stories, you couldn't fit them all in just one notebook, I'd need several volumes to tell the tales of all these accursed kings, so there was the Printer, all eager to talk, and I just went on staring into my glass of red wine like a philosopher wondering what deep, dark secret a liquid might conceal, and let me tell you a secret right now, if you want people to talk you have to stand back, feign indifference, pretend, in a word, not to care, it's the oldest and best strategy in the world for setting things in motion, people looking to confess get upset then, they think their story the most extraordinary, most astonishing, the weirdest, most surprising, most action-packed ever told, and they want to get you to believe the tale they're going to tell is of a gravity and seriousness equaled only by the death penalty itself, "why d'you want to talk to me," I made out I was surprised, when in fact I did want to hear him, and he replied "because people say you're a good guy," and I laughed, then lifted my glass of red and drank from it, "and what have they told you about me?" I asked the Printer, "they say you're the top man around here," and I laughed again, then told him *"if wisdom could be measured by inches of beard, billy goats would be philosophers,"* the Printer stared at me and leaning toward me said "why you talking like that, Broken Glass, I'm looking for someone to understand me, what's all this stuff about billy goats and philosophers?" and I told him to calm down, I was taking him seriously, and I added, "they must have said other things, what else did they say about me?" and he nodded "yeah, they said you were in here right at the start, that the Stubborn Snail's a close personal friend, that he listens to what you say," I smiled, flattered by these kind words, I like to hear things like that, the guy began to interest me, "and what else, they must have said something else," and he thought for a moment, casting his eyes upward, "well, it seems you're writing something about the people who come here, you're keeping a notebook, it must be that one there beside you, is it?" and I didn't answer, just placed my hand over the notebook where it lay open, because the guy was trying to read my scribble, I don't like that, and I gave the bottle a good shake and poured myself another glass, and drank it off then asked him "so what is it you want then?" and he suddenly raised his voice saying "I want to be in your notebook too, you're going to make some assholes famous when actually I'm the most interesting case round here," some arrogance, who did he think he was then, "okay, okay, calm down, so what makes you think you're so interesting, then, you got no grounds to say that, just give me one reason, go on, just one, why you're more interesting than anyone else around here" and he said, without hesitation, "I'm more important than the rest because I've been to France, not everyone can say that, believe me" and he said it quite naturally, as though it was obvious, France was his yardstick, the height of achievement, he'd set foot in France, therefore he was always going to be right, well, what could I say, after that, I tried to think of a counterargument, but none sprang to mind, so I capitulated and said "okay, then, sit down, my friend, let's hear what you have to say," and he sat down at my table and filled up the empty glass he'd just taken from the neighboring table and drank from it, and cleared his throat three times, before warning me "I'm telling you, Broken Glass, if you don't put me into your book, it won't be worth the paper it's written on, I tell you, they could make my life into a film," and eventually he calmed down and there was a long silence in which we listened to drunken angels drifting overhead, and I kept on looking at him "okay, where shall I start, what comes first," he said, in a resigned sort of voice, and I said nothing, and he went on "to be honest, I don't hate the French—men or women, but I do hate one French woman, just one, I swear" which was good for a beginning, I like that kind of statement, so I just kept up my silence, I wanted him to come out with it now, I bore down on him with my eyes, and he brought out his big artillery, saying "ah, France, don't talk to me about France, Broken Glass, it makes me want to vomit" and he spat on the ground, and his face went hard like the face of a gorilla who's seen a poacher cross his patch "okay, I'll start at the very beginning, but listen carefully, what I'm telling you now is important, very important, so you pay attention, I want to see you writing while I talk, and you'll see, you should never ever trust anyone, I'm telling you that as a friend, Broken Glass," he really knew how to spin it out, I wanted to tell him to get to the point and stop dithering around in the penalty area, and while I was scribbling down some of what he'd begun to say he said "in fact I'm going to tell you about a woman, how she killed me, ruined me, reduced me to a piece of nonrecyclable rubbish, so she did" and I leaned over toward him and he moved back a few centimeters, as though to keep some distance between us, I didn't see why, and he said "Broken Glass, don't mess with white women, if you ever cross paths with a white woman, go your own way, don't even look on her, she'll stop at nothing, I don't even know how I came to be back here, when my place is in Europe, in France, and here I am, either in this bar or on the beaches of the Côte Sauvage" and he took a drink of his red wine and wiped his mouth with his bare hand and went on "to tell you the truth, it's her fault I drink like I do, the white witch's fault, she sucked out my blood, Broken Glass, believe me, I was a decent man, I don't know if you understand what's meant by a decent man in France, but I was a man who earned his living, a man who paid his income tax on time, a man with a post office savings account, a man who even had shares on the stock exchange in Paris, a man who was saving for his pension in France—because pensions in this country are nothing but a pile of shit, a road to ruin, unreliable, a lottery, you need to have some cushy job in a ministry, there are civil servants in this country who do business with the pensions of poor people who've worked all their lives, but anyway, I was somebody in the black community back there, people knew me, I was a worker, a real hard worker, not a layabout like some black immigrants who hang around in the lobbies of their apartments, waiting for the family support checks, I didn't need all that shit, no, yours truly worked in a large print works on the outskirts of Paris, I ran my own section, I even hired and fired the other guys, because I could tell a lazy sod from a hard worker, and I didn't just hire negroes either, because, between you and me, Broken Glass, there's more to life than negroes, for fuck's sake, there are other races too, negroes don't have a monopoly on misery, or on unemployment, I also hired miserable, unemployed people with white skin, and yellow skin, I mixed them all up together, just so you know, I had real status, and not every black gets to hire and fire white men, who, after all, were the ones who colonized them, Christianized them, flung them into the holds of ships, whipped them and trampled them, burned their gods, put down their rebellions, wiped out their empires, so I hired people with white skin and people with yellow skin, and I mixed them together with the other wretched of the earth, and there weren't many Negroes doing that, you could count us on the fingers of a fatwa victim, check it out, anyone will tell you, so there I was with a good job, a well-paid job, we printed *Paris Match*, *VSD*, *Voici*, *Figaro*, *Les Echos*, I was a decent man, I was married to Céline, a woman from Vendée with a terrific ass on her, an ass like a real negress's from back home and Céline was secretary to the head of a pharmaceutical lab in Colombes," and at this point in his confession I began to wonder if the Printer wasn't having me on, but he spoke with such assurance I had to believe him, and he went on "I should tell you I first met Céline at Timis, a well known black nightclub in Pigalle, in the Eighteenth Arrondissement of Paris, I don't know what she was doing there, surrounded by vulgar black women in heat, even if you could make out the odd other white woman among them, but the other whites were all lumbered with backsides as flat as an ironing board, and Céline immediately caught my eye, with her butt and her waist, and the two great big watermelons grafted onto her chest, so that no one else dared approach her on the dance floor, and I just went straight up to her like a soldier who's just been given a medal, I crossed the Rubicon murmuring to myself "*alea iacta est*" and without a flicker of hesitation I plunged in there, praying that it would all run smoothly because the worst thing for a man trying to get a girl to dance is being turned down in the middle of the dance floor in front of the competition, who all piss themselves laughing, anyway, thank God, I was well dressed, I had on a dress shirt by Christian Dior that I bought in the rue du Faubourg-Saint-Honoré and an Yves Saint Laurent blazer I'd got in the rue Matignon, and some lizard-skin Weston shoes I got somewhere near the Place de la Madeleine and I wore this really good perfume called The Male by Jean-Paul Gaultier that I'd mixed together with Lolita Lempika for men, and as for my haircut, it was pure black American actor at the height of his success, Sydney Poitier style, so all in all I was okay, I was in good shape, I held out my hand to the girl, who'd been dancing and was now sitting on the velour-covered pouf finishing off a cigarette as long and slim as a reed in a sweeping brush, and the girl stood up at once, as though she had been waiting for this moment, my heart began leaping and bounding, I couldn't quite believe it, I saw the disappointment in the faces of the competition, knowing they'd lost a fine chance this time, I told myself I'd better give it my all, dance as I'd never danced before, and make a once-in-a-lifetime impression on this girl, so that she'd be the one left asking for more, and we danced all night and then, you won't believe this, Broken Glass, she came back to my place, no discussion, none of your 'well, we've only just met, I need some time, let's get to know each other, I'm not one of those girls who open their legs on the first date, I need to talk about it, let's have a coffee, meet up a few times, then we'll see,' no, none of that, she just came back to my place without getting all fancy about it and I was in my Renault 19, and she drove behind in her Toyota, and when we got to my place we parked outside the building and kissed in the corridor and in the elevator, and on the landing, and in front of my door, which I couldn't get open because I was actually drunk as a skunk, and I didn't waste any time, we got down on the carpet and I made a really thorough job of it, I worked on her from every angle, under every layer of her haute couture, and there we lay entwined at dawn, a little dazed by the speed of things, but so what, it was so good, we soon got over that, and Céline left, saying she'd had a wonderful evening, the best evening ever in her whole life, and I was a really nice guy and she took my phone number and I took hers, and since days are long and nights are short we called each other regularly, for hours on end, we exchanged the latest details of the night, we said a whole heap of stupid things, the kind of stupid things lovers come out with when love is new, so I had to tell her I loved her, had to be open with my feelings, had to express them without reserve, she told me, and that was the first time I really learned how to tell a woman I loved her, not like here where you don't say it because you don't want to seem weak, here you get your rocks off at night, don't bother with the romantic fairy-tale stuff, but it's different in France, they take feelings seriously there, you don't play games with love, and very soon I made the marriage proposal she'd been waiting for since the day we met, she said she knew instinctively I was the man she'd spend the rest of her life with, as though God had said we should be one, and Céline quickly talked her parents round, they're not racists, they always voted Communist in municipal and regional elections, or for the Greens in the presidential, so we went to visit them in some little place in Vendée called Noirmoutier, an island with a bridge connecting it to the mainland, and Céline's parents said I was a fine young man, distinguished, intelligent, refined, ambitious, respectful of republican values, and I was pleased to hear this description of my noble qualities, they admired the way I was dressed, which isn't surprising because I was actually wearing a made-to-measure Francesco Smalto suit, and they also said how they loved deepest Africa, the real Africa, mysterious Africa, the bush, the red earth, the wild animals skipping about in the wide open spaces, adding that only fools thought that black Africa was heading for disaster, or that Africa was antidevelopment and they apologized personally for the mistakes of the past, in particular for the slave trade, colonization, the problems with independence and all the other shit some black fundamentalists have made their thing, I didn't want to get into those worn-out arguments, I made it clear to them that stuff to do with the past was not my thing, I was a man with my eyes fixed firmly on the horizon, and that horizon was not aflame, I said I was looking to the future, then I began talking to them about the Congo, and they asked which Congo I was from originally, the father asked if it was the Belgian Congo, the mother asked if it was the French Congo, and I said the Belgian Congo no longer existed, and I said the French Congo no longer existed, I explained that I was from the Republic of the Congo, i.e., the smaller of the two Congos, and the father exclaimed 'of course he's from the little Congo, our beautiful, illustrious former colony, General de Gaulle even declared Brazzaville the capital of free France during the occupation, ah, the Congo, land of dreams and freedom, it's the country where they speak the purest French, you know, better even than in France, let me tell you,' and Céline's mother, who was a bit embarrassed, told her husband he shouldn't be using the word *colony* in reference to my country, "now then, Joseph," she said, "it doesn't do to say *colony*, you know that," and the father said it was a mistake and what he meant was *territory* and the mother said that *colony* and *territory* were completely interchangeable and Céline flew into a rage and said we hadn't come to talk about interchanges or geography or history, and old father Joseph said 'good, let's drink to that with a decent bottle of claret, shall we' and he opened the claret and we drank, and seeing as how the atmosphere was now relaxed, Céline and I announced our imminent nuptials and the father was caught short by this and almost choked on his wine and said 'you don't hang about do you, you young ones, in our day you had to take your time about it, get to know the family, what is it you want, a TGV marriage, or what?' and Céline's mother kicked her husband under the table then said 'love is love, you know that Joseph,' and they gave us their blessing despite everything, since Céline wouldn't have allowed them to say no anyway, it was take it or leave it, and her parents came to Paris for the happy day, there were only about fifty or so of us, in a little registry office in Chatenay-Malabry, some friends of Celine's, my work colleagues, and a few acquaintances, most of them Sappers, and when I say 'Sappers,' my dear Broken Glass, I do not mean the guys who put out fires, no, Sappers are boys from the black milieu in Paris, who belong to SAPPE which is the Society for Ambience and People and Persons of Elegance, and among the Sappers present that day were influential guys like Djo Ballard and Docteur Limane, Michel Macchabée, Moulé Moulé, Moki, Benos, Préfet and a load of others"

"I hope you've been noting down what I'm telling you, I was up to where we'd got married, we now had our whole lives in front of us, we now had to work out where we were going and what we wanted, and as we both had good jobs we decided straight away to take out a mortgage on a large house, a nice, proper detached house, in the comfortable suburbs, half an hour from Paris because we wanted a pleasant life, and above all a life well away from negroes, I'm no racist, but believe me, the worst enemy of mixed-race couples isn't always the white next door, it's usually a black, no really, I'm not racist, Broken Glass, I'm just telling you the facts, if people don't agree with me, they can keep their moral judgments to themselves, to hell with them, not that I'm going to sit down and write a Letter to Black France to lay the blame on anyone, in fact if other negroes see you with a white woman they think they can get off with her too, they think if a normal sane white woman is shacked up with some gorilla from the Congo, she might as well get shacked up with the whole wildlife park, the entire reservation, you know what I mean, anyway, let it drop, I'm not here to rub salt intó the open wounds of my race, my race is what it is, the fact is, Céline and I wanted to live well away from the hubbub of Paris and the envy of other negroes, and the whole classic comedy, we thought that privacy would bring happiness, and it was a fine life we lived, a *vie en rose*, with our two daughters, twins born two years after we got married, little mixed-race girls with blue eyes, believe me, ours was the best of lives, we were a model couple, even if the mean-mouthed blacks back in Paris were always saying that black–white couples never last long, you never see husband and wife grow old together, and that it will only last if the black guy gives up being black, and changes altogether, does an about turn, makes concessions, denies his own people three times before the cock crows, turns his back on his overdependent family, in short, if he keeps his black skin but wears a white mask, whereas our marriage was a good one, Broken Glass, I couldn't imagine anything coming to spoil it, I didn't need to wear a white mask to hide my black skin, I was actually proud to be a black, I always will be, till my dying day, I'm proud of my black culture, you know what I mean, Céline respected me for that, everything was going fine, I was a good father to my family, the sky was blue with little brightly colored birds in it, hopping from branch to branch in the trees outside our house, which I had painted green, a color I'm very fond of, which is why the neighbors called it "the green house" and everything was going swimmingly, Broken Glass, and when the sky is too blue, like that, you have to remember that one day something might come along and turn it grey, if the sun shines too brightly it can kill your love, and that's what I was about to find out to my cost"

"then one day our bright blue sky clouded over, the little birds with their multicolored feathers flew away without a goodbye, and the next morning they didn't turn up to sing in the dawn, and birds of ill omen, birds with heavy wings came to replace them, cawing and pecking with their wizened beaks at the tree trunk of our deep-rooted union, this was the time when the whole story of my son came out, who I'd had with a West Indian woman when I first arrived in France, and I was still studying at the Centre National des Arts et Métiers, now this West Indian woman was threatening me with a lawsuit because I owed her four years' maintenance and all that stuff, and I went on a counterattack with all the force of a bull seeking to cut short the spectacle the aficionados hope for, I got myself a good female lawyer who was able to show that in fact it was the West Indian woman who was preventing me from fulfilling my obligations as a father, I managed to get my son to come and live with us because I wanted to take charge of his education myself and give him a future, there was room enough in our nice green house, Céline agreed with me, had even encouraged me, saying blood was thicker than water and I shouldn't abandon my offspring like an irresponsible father, so that's how I played it, my son came to live with us, but unfortunately he fell in with the local riffraff and I did my best to get him back on track but it was no use, he yelled at me, wanted nothing to do with the fine future I was offering him, he tried to attack me, can you believe, and I was suddenly all at sea, since when did a child raise his hand against his father, but I knew he despised me, I could tell, he'd never been able to accept my leaving his mother and marrying Céline, especially since she was white, he said I'd been bought, that I'd gone over to the other side, I was a Banania black, I was all fucked up, just a slave to white meat and pig's trotters, it was pretty awful actually, but he was my son, after all, and what really riled me was when he came and announced that he'd seen Céline with some local Africans, and one of them, called Ferdinand, was my wife's lover, now that really did upset me seriously, I took it he was just trying to wind me up because Céline would never dare do anything like that to me, she knew what I thought about other blacks, even if I'm not racist, I want you to know that, so anyway, my son was just a first-class liar, I told myself, and I decided to ignore it, I reckoned it was just another of his little outbursts, and I didn't even check it out, it seemed so obviously made-up, it's true I didn't keep a tight rein on Céline, I let her get on with her own life, you don't mess with a white woman's personal freedom, she takes it seriously, I was more relaxed than in the early days of our marriage, I let her go out with her girlfriends, and sometimes I even looked after the children while I wasn't at work, that was how we managed things, now, stay with me here Broken Glass, this is where it starts getting interesting, one day my heart practically stops beating when I find a condom floating in the toilet in our green house, a really big condom, about twice the size of my own dick, which is itself enormous, I can show you if you like, so I thought it must be my son who'd brought back some local white slut, or maybe a black one, though I had warned him not to, even if he was eighteen already, what would have happened if he'd got some girl pregnant, eh, where did he think he'd find the money to look after a poor kid, that's the kind of thing I was thinking, I couldn't imagine my son having it off with a girl, it just wasn't possible, I'd never seen him show any interest in a girl, I even wondered whether he might not be a bit slow, sexually, but you should never take anything as certain, you should never think that just because a kid is quiet they'll never do something dreadful, and I also thought that it was pretty disrespectful toward me to give rein to his basest impulses in the family home, if you see what I mean, Broken Glass, so while I was thinking it over, with the image of this enormous condom fixed in my head, like some image from a surrealist painting, I started get weird ideas about things, I stopped sleeping at night, I thought maybe someone had been in the house, Céline's lover, perhaps, or maybe the local African guy, this Ferdinand my son had mentioned, and at that point I saw red, I could see everything falling apart, my happiness gone, it didn't make sense for some devil to come and screw up everything in my private paradise, I was way out of control, I considered murder—with a knife, a screwdriver, an axe, a hammer, Céline was no longer my Céline, she felt dirty, debased, impure, criminal, I would have to kill her and her lover, the two of them, I was sure she was the one who'd gone running after said Ferdinand, wiggling her ass in that obscene way of hers, I'd have to kill them both together, set an ambush for them, it's not hard to catch a white woman who's two-timing you with a negro, you just have to say something insulting about Africa and negroes, that all negroes are starving, mud-hut-dwelling idle good-for-nothings with their civil wars and their machete brawls, and a white woman will instantly give herself away, but I decided it wasn't a good idea to go down that route with her, I'd look like a racist, however justified, and besides, I had no proof, so I let the incident pass, and life went on as usual, I was angry with myself for being so paranoid, things were okay, though I still couldn't understand how that condom came to be in my house, and since God always has one eye open, after a few days of deceptive calm I found another huge Manix condom floating in the bidet because the problem with condoms is, you think you've got rid of them by flushing them down the toilet, but then they pop back up again, and this time I decided I wouldn't just ignore it, I'm not stupid, after all, I wasn't prepared to just give them the green light, say "after you, Africans!" so they could come and screw my wife in my own private shag-o-drome, I opted for the high-risk strategy of direct action, I would conduct my own investigation, like a real detective, I wasn't going to let my entire life be poisoned by a Manix condom, I needed a proper investigation, to understand exactly what was going on in my house while I was out, I decided, so one day, a Monday, a grey Monday morning, I told Céline I was going to work and I'd be back very late as we had a new magazine to get out in the next twenty-four hours and she swallowed my story because I never lied to her, never ever, I was always straight with her, I left the house, took the car and went and hung around in town for an hour, drinking bitter coffee and smoking like a chimney, I called work and said I was taking the day off because of a serious family matter, and I knocked back my coffee like water, I even picked up a half bottle of gin, because I needed to be in another world at the moment when I caught Céline with this Ferdinand guy—who had the nerve to come and prey on me as I imbibed my humble beverage—and there in that little bar, I kept rerunning the film of our first meeting in my head, I saw her once again, the night we met at Timis, drenched in sweat, kissing me, I saw us once more in the lift, and on the carpet, heard her screams of pleasure, and in a sudden burst of rage I banged my fist on the steering wheel and set off the horn, and I bit my lower lip and said to myself 'what if she screams with pleasure when she's making love with this Ferdinand?' and I said to myself, 'deep down I'm just a poor saddo, till now I always thought I was the only one who could send her to seventh heaven, now some bastard negro brother comes along, maybe he's better than me, maybe he sends her to eighth or ninth heaven, well we'll find out this evening,' and I got back to our neighborhood thinking all these black thoughts and I parked several blocks from our house, and said a quick prayer, it was almost six o'clock in the evening, I walked about for a few minutes, the green house was just a few yards off, I went through the yard and then, as I'd had too much to drink, I had a job tiptoeing through to our bedroom, I kept bumping into things, but it didn't matter, I was getting there, I saw the door was slightly open, I pushed it, there was no one inside, so I crept down the main corridor, that goes through the dining room, till I got to my older son's room, my heart was pounding, part of me wanted to know the truth, part of me was terrified, and I heard some sort of rumpus coming from inside the room, laughter, and a bed creaking, then moaning, the sound of a whip lashing, and suddenly I bounded forward and the door opened like in a Columbo or a Maigret film, and there, Broken Glass, bet you won't believe me, I saw Céline and my son in the bed, all tangled up in the poor Christ of Bomba position, but Céline was the one on top of my son, holding the whip, and they were drenched in sweat, the sheets were on the floor, I swear to you, Broken Glass, I immediately let out a scream like the cry of a mad bird, *yaaaahhhhhhhhhhh*, I didn't know what to do, I just stood there shaking, the world seemed to come crashing down at my feet, then I lunged at my son and flung him to the floor so I could cut his throat, but he flipped me over and punched me in the guts and as I tried to get up, Céline, who was over on the other side of the room, screaming, came to his aid, then the two of them pushed me up against the wall, I was too drunk to put up a proper fight against two adversaries whose flesh had been joined in the act of original sin, and my son set about me with the whip they used for their disgusting sport, then punched me in the guts and in the head, honestly, all over, Broken Glass, and then I passed out and they called the police, and they told the police I'd gone mad and my two daughters, who were playing out in the backyard were crying, Broken Glass, and I swear to you, when I woke up the next morning I didn't know what was going on, I was in some kind of madhouse, an asylum, yeah, an asylum where time passed really slowly and people dressed in white coats were in constant attendance, pushing me round in a wheelchair like an *Australopithecus*, and they'd shaved my head and bound my hands because they were afraid I'd smash the place up, and the other inmates were all making fun of me saying 'hey guys, come and listen to this one, look at that lunatic over there, never stops shouting, thinks his kid's screwing his wife, heh, heh, he really is crazy,' and they put me in the special section for dangerous lunatics who spend the whole day shouting, so I did start shouting, because in the special bit for dangerous lunatics you have to shout or the other lunatics beat you up, and I tried to explain that I wasn't mad, my older son was screwing my wife, that my Nether Regions were his Nether Regions, that I had come across my wife and my son naked, naked as earthworms, one on top of the other in the poor Christ of Bomba position, and I said they even had a whip and my wife was the one holding the whip, like someone practicing philosophy in the boudoir, I heard people laughing in every corner, and that was when a negro woman in a white coat came up and gave me a glass of water which, on a sudden impulse, I upset, which sent my wheelchair hurtling down to the far end of the main room of the building, and the chief doctor came running up, followed by at least a half-dozen nurses, and I heard the chief doctor order, with all the lofty authority bestowed by his State doctorate in psychiatry, 'tighten his restraints, I told you not to leave him alone for a second, we'll double his medication, give him a jab, that'll quiet him down once and for all for God's sake' and then gave me a jab to send me to sleep because they reckoned I was delirious, repeating the same thing over and over, they thought I'd made up the story about my wife and my son, because Céline told anyone who would listen that I'd gone off my head, I was a drunkard, I beat up my son, who had of course backed up Céline's lies, and so I was given an injection to stop the ranting and raving, and I must have slept for a long time, because when I woke up I couldn't remember anything, I really thought I must have died and gone to heaven, because there were clouds everywhere, and butterflies of a thousand different colors fluttering about at low altitude, so I said I wanted to speak to God in person, not to his angels, I said I'd only speak in the presence of God the Father, and all these angels and other celestial underlings could fuck off, and they looked at me askance and told me to calm down, they said God the Father would be ready to receive me shortly, that was the plan, I had made it to paradise, and then I saw before me a black man the size of a sculpture by Ousmane Sow, no longer young, dressed in a white coat, he walked in solemnly, like someone about to say mass, and told me he was God Almighty and I started like a young goat when I heard that, I became angry and said that was a serious insult, an unpardonable heresy, I said this guy was not God, no way, I said God was not black, and they all looked at me very shocked and sent for another man in a white coat, and he was tall too, also with grey hair, and a thick beard, blue eyes, and very white skin, and I felt myself going into a real trance, with real shuddering and shaking, like I was possessed by the Holy Spirit, and I began to speak as though I were talking to God himself and after my confession my voice suddenly failed me, I couldn't say another word, I'd gone quite mad, I tell you, I couldn't speak, and everyone began to look blurred, and I felt like there was constant noise all around me, and everyone was talking too loud, and my wife didn't visit me, nor did my son, and I didn't even recognize the colleagues who visited me with flowers and the latest issue of *Paris Match*, and I insulted them all so badly that after a month they all stopped coming to see me in the asylum, and my wife went to see an African lawyer from this country to ask for a divorce, who better to defend her than some guy from my own place, a guy who was born in this very neighborhood, I tell you, and I'm quite sure that shit of a no-good lawyer got down dirty in bed with Céline, because the minute she has a black man in front of her she has to get her teeth into him, I swear to you, she knows how to make love to a negro without getting tired, she got her divorce, apparently the law was quite clear on that point, she had no obligation to stick with a nutter who was known to be dangerous, a husband who wasn't right in the head, page and paragraph number whatever of the Code civil of 1804, so she was given custody of the children, and most importantly she got me repatriated, helped by the fact that my family back home had been asking for the same thing ever since they heard about the whole unpleasant episode, and in the months leading up to my return I still said nothing, in fact I only recovered my senses the day the plane landed, when I saw my entire family gathered together, the sadness and the shame in their eyes, believe me, they were not happy, so then I started drinking, to get away from the ghosts that were haunting me, I refused to live with my parents, that humiliation I did refuse, and I started to walk, day and night, which is how I came to be here now, bowed and bent like an old man, I roam the shore, I talk with the ghosts that haunt me, and in the afternoons I come here, unfortunately, but tell me honestly, Broken Glass, in your heart of hearts, do you also think I'm mad, do you think I'm an idiot, do I sound to you like a madman, talking the usual rubbish people talk, go on, tell me the truth, promise me you'll put down what I've told you in your book, you won't tear up what you've written there, let me tell you again, if you don't put all that in your book it'll be worthless, completely worthless, you do know, don't you, out of all the guys who come here, I'm the most important, and I'll tell you why, because I've done France, that's why, and it's not every idiot who can say he's done France"

I come across the Printer every day now, spilling out his story to someone or other, what he calls his ambiguous adventure, though he made out to me I was the only person he'd ever told, I do think there's something not right in his head, sometimes what he says makes perfect sense, especially in the afternoons, but I really think this story's scrambled his head

I like chatting with the boss of Credit Gone West, everyone knows he's not married, and has no children, he thinks all that's just a burden, that it's not easy being a married man, too many problems, too much bother, that's why he often says he's married for life to Credit Gone West, has been already for many years now, and it's true that sometimes he's been seen disappearing upstairs with a woman, often a well-endowed woman, flat-chested women don't interest him, so yes, sometimes, he's been seen to shut himself in up there, and then come back down again later all out of breath, a smile on his face, and then we'd all know that the Stubborn Snail just got laid, then suddenly he'd get wildly generous and buy a drink for anyone who asked, sometimes I glimpsed his aged parents, back from Ngolobondo, his native village, the Stubborn Snail and his father are like two peas in a pod, but he never said anything to us about his parents, I know they're alive, they must be even older and wearier by now, but they chose to go back and live in their village after the whole controversy over the creation of their son's bar broke out, people who were close to them say they love their only son, and did everything to enable him to go to school and get a job in an office or become a full-time civil servant, but things turned out differently, fate chose otherwise, I don't mean the Stubborn Snail was a dunce at school, he was at school with the present agriculture minister, Albert Zou Loukia, so no, the boss of Credit Gone West was no dunce at school, far from it, it's even been said he was brilliant, a quite brilliant pupil, he loved dissertations, geography, arithmetic, all that jazz, and he can still recite whole poems from memory, without a single hesitation, which really blows my mind, I've often tried it myself, but I never get beyond two verses, and our boss particularly loves "The Death of the Wolf," by Alfred de Vigny, he's always reciting that, and when I hear the last verse it always brings tears to my eyes, you'd think this Alfred de Vigny guy had written the words in advance especially for him, you should hear the Stubborn Snail when he murmurs "groaning, weeping, praying –these are the coward's way, / With energy and strength face your long and heavy task, / Tread the path which Destiny has called you to, / Then, like me, suffer and die in silence," he recalls proudly how he got his baccalaureate at the first attempt, he could have studied further, but, alas, without warning his parents, he gave up his studies, which was the thing to do at the time, you had to go abroad and make your mark there, those were the years of the lean cattle back then, high-up people were already finding jobs for their relatives, however incompetent, and the Stubborn Snail began to work his way round Angola, Gabon, and Chad, he had always wanted to be a businessman, answerable to no one, and in the end it was during the trip to Cameroon that he got the idea of setting up his bar, with all the repercussions I described earlier, I won't go back over all that because even when I'm drunk I hate useless repetition or padding, as used by certain writers known to be first-class drivelers, who serve up the same old stuff in every new book and try to make out they've created a world, my eye "how about you, Broken Glass, how are things with you these days?" the Stubborn Snail asked me a few days ago, not for the first time, "oh, not too bad" I replied, and he said, seriously, Broken Glass, I think what you need is a bit of affection, you should find yourself a nice girlfriend, get laid once in a while, it would really do you good," "I don't see the point at my age," I replied, "I tell you, you need to start over, age has nothing to do with it," "no, who'd take on a wreck like me, you'd better be kidding, Stubborn Snail," "I'm not, I'm quite serious, what would you say to Robinette, then, she's a juicy mouthful, don't you think?" he went on, "my God, not Robinette, she's more than a mouthful for me, I'd never manage to swallow her!" I said, and I started laughing, and we both laughed, I'd just remembered Robinette's last appearance at Credit Gone West, the boss was trying to hitch me up with a real iron lady, I thought he must be joking because Robinette drinks more than I do, she drinks like those barrels of Adelaide wine that the Lebanese sell at the Grand Marché, Robinette drinks and drinks, and never gets drunk, and when she drinks like that she goes to piss behind the bar instead of in the bathroom like everyone else, and when she pisses behind the bar she can urinate nonstop for ten minutes, it just flows and flows as though someone had turned on a public fountain, and it's not a trick, it's incredible, but true, men have tried to compete with her at endurance pissing, but have been forced to say farewell to arms, defeated, crushed, wiped out, mocked, rolled in the dust, in cornstarch

the last time Robinette dropped by, she came on to a guy we'd never seen before at Credit Gone West, it began with a direct attack from Robinette, the kind of invisible blow dealt by Muhammed Ali to Sonny Liston in the sixties, when he was defending his world-champion title, "hey you there, strutting about like a barnyard cock, if you can piss longer than me I'll let you shag me, any time, any place, free of charge, I give you my word" she said, and the guy replied "show off, you don't know what you're taking on, I accept your challenge, Robinette, but I'm going to give you a proper going-over when we're done, I like a fat ass with big tits," and we all laughed, because the guy was truly a first-class braggart, he had no idea what he was up against, if he'd known the first thing about her he would have thought twice about what he was saying, there we all were, killing ourselves laughing, imagining the fellow's corpse already, flat out on the ground, and the newcomer's words certainly irritated Robinette, the inconquerable, the piss queen of the town, of the neighborhood, so she answered "are you mad, or what, my boy, before you start calling me fat, you win your contest, you're just talking rubbish, no way you're gonna beat me, not the way I see you standing here, Mr. All Mouth and No Trousers," "oh yes I am gonna beat you, my fat lady," says he, "oh no you're not you jumped-up midget, you gotta be mad to try and beat me at my game, you ask any of these guys here, they'll tell you who you're up against" answered Robinette, "I'm no braggart darling, you'll find I always do what I say I'm gonna do," he riposted, "you boaster, you, you think just because you talk smart like that you can do just anything you say you can do, I say you can't do nothing" said Robinette, and from where I was watching, some way off, I thought it must be a joke, that they knew each other already, and we were being treated to a brief scene from *Three Suitors, One Husband*, some hilarious farce, at any rate, I thought they really must be thick as any two thieves in this town, weird kind of people, but no, it wasn't a play at all, and the boasting guy was actually putting up a brave show, an unknown on the circuit, unaware of what was waiting round the next river bend, dressed like a man of substance, in his black jacket, white shirt, red tie, and polished shoes, what did he take us for, beggars, bumpkins, in short, a band of workers of the world who wouldn't unite, and we couldn't figure how he'd got his hair, which he'd straightened and fastened behind at the neck, to shine so bright in this dry white season, when the August sunshine barely shone through the layer of cloud, but a peacock's a peacock whatever the season, it still struts and preens in the dry white season, the fact was, even at dead of night, this guy's hair would still have shone as bright as it shone that day, he must spend hours in front of the mirror, the straightening iron was his fetish, in a country where frizzy hair is the greatest of curses his own straight hair brought him just that little bit closer to the white man, and he smoked a lot, in an elegant way, and he introduced himself to people, saying "for those who don't know, my first name is Casimir, I am Casimir, the unstoppable, known far and wide, I live the high life, you know, I've only stopped off here for a quick drink, that's all, I'm not an old soak like the rest of you, it's the high life for me" and I said to myself, "holy shit, who is this guy, shooting his mouth off, does he understand what kind of Vietnam he's signing himself up for here?" and we all felt pretty antagonistic toward this Casimir, boasting about his high life, and calling us sad old soaks, why didn't he go somewhere else for a drink, then, with all the high lifers, eh, why turn up here to remind us we were nothing but wretched upstarts, Robinette was right to say he was talking rubbish, I reckoned the guy deserved a good lesson, a bit of proper punishment, and I said to myself "in any case, so be it, the chips are down" else what's he think he's doing here, in his fancy get-up, like a lawyer, or an undertaker, or an opera maestro, opera being the pain-in-the-ass sort of music that people living the high life like Casimir like to listen to and applaud, even though they don't understand a word of it, what kind of music is it that that you can't even wiggle your butt to, when you can't even say to the people around you "watch me dance!" what kind of music is it, if it doesn't make you sweat, and rub at a woman's love mound, to bring her mind round to the fatal act, but when I used to dance, I mean, when I was still a man like other men, I liked to get myself into the kind of state where I felt like I was floating down into paradise, seeing those drunken angels carry me on their wings, I was a good dancer, when I could put my partner in such a spin she'd collapse in my arms and let me decide how the night proceeded, but I'm not ready just yet to talk about myself in case you think I'm some ego-tripper with his nose stuck fast in his naval, so anyway, Robinette and this guy disappear round the back of Credit Gone West to fight out the war of the end of the world, and out the back of Credit Gone West there's a sort of cul-de-sac, the perfect setting for a wide variety of lewd sexual acts, where people come from far and wide to do their dodgy business, and where our two contestants now withdrew to, followed by the rest of us, as eyewitnesses, as voyeurs, really, eager to see Casimir, he of the high life, take his tumble, and learn a little humility at last, and keep his mouth shut in company, we were all on Robinette's side, cheering her on, applauding her efforts, and so, out the back of Credit Gone West, in a grubby corner stinking of cat's piss and mad-cow dung, Casimir, he of the high life, slipped off his old man's jacket and his medal, took off his fluttering tie, carefully folded up his things, put the whole lot down on the ground in a corner, then—ultimate piece of vanity, which really irritated us—checked his face in his polished shoes, who did he think he was then, asshole, why was he peering at himself when his mashed-up fig face was about to get another pounding when Robinette had finished making a fool of him, but there he was, preening away, running his hand over his hair, which he'd smoothed with a straightening iron, and which shone even in the pale August sunlight, we'd never seen a guy so full of himself, so first of all, Robinette took off her bodice wrap, which was not exactly a sight to rival La Reine Margot unhooking her corset, then she lifted her skirt wrap to just below her waist so we could see her great big behind, like a perissodactyl mammal's, her huge plump thighs like those of a woman in a naive Haitian painting, her calves like bottles of Primus beer, she wore no panties, naughty girl, perhaps because no panties exist large enough to contain her mountainous cheeks, then, after a long, repellent belch, she raised her voice and said "God willing, the truth will be revealed at the first light of dawn, to have and have not, that is what we are about to discover, my friends," and then as she parted the twin towers of her buttocks we saw her sex, and all applauded, and curiously, I and all the other witnesses at once got huge erections, I'm being honest here, I'm trying to speak the truth, yeah, I got an erection simply because a woman's backside is a woman's backside, be it small, large, flat, or fat, striped like a zebra's, splashed with neuralgia-inducing pigments or palm-wine stains, or pox scars, a woman's backside is a woman's backside, first you get a hard-on, then you decide if you're going to go for it or if you're not, so then we all watched Casimir High-Life take off his trousers, revealing his little legs, skinny as a wader bird's, and knees like a web of Gordian knots, he was wearing tomato-red pants, which he pulled down to his ankles, and there was his sex, his original indivisible element, at which we all burst out laughing, and wondering where his puny piss would come from, but there he stood, calmly displaying this insignificant object, with its hairy appendages hanging down like the fruit of a breadfruit tree at the end of a dry white season, and began to knead his original indivisible element, handling it like a greasy pole, talking to it quietly, like a snake charmer before a crowd of tourists in the marketplace, he settled down to the serious task of getting it into a catholic shape, which was no easy task with all these people looking on in derision, all supporting Robinette, no easy task at all, with them all trying to put him off by whatever means possible, because of his feeble little member, but he concentrated hard, as though we didn't exist, aware that he was on his own here, that the rest of us were all for Robinette, but it didn't shake his confidence, far from it, he had a kind of calm assurance, paid no attention to his opponent, went about his preparations with the serenity of a professional in this kind of contest, and he shook his original indivisible element, and tugged at it and twisted it this way and that, summoning up his urine, and then suddenly off he went, *whoosh*, we were off, the contest had started, Robinette spread wide her elephantine legs, her entire Nether Regions now smack in our faces, and we certainly saw her sweet little pea begin to swell and suddenly there she was, giving out an animal squeal, like a hyena giving birth, we almost got sprayed with the steaming yellow liquid, spurting like a sac of water that's suddenly been pierced, we just managed to step back in time, while in the other corner Casimir High-Life was liberating the contents of his bladder, but Robinette's stream was heavier, hotter, more majestic, and above all had a longer range, while her cocky opponent's came out in little fits and starts, like a baby kangaroo, a frog hoping to turn into a bull cow, a crow emulating an eagle, it wiggled and staggered and zigzagged about, tracing strange hieroglyphics on the ground, enough to give a headache to that guy they called Champollion, who enjoyed racking his brains over those drawings that look like they've been done by a three-year-old from the time of the pharaohs and other mummies, and this guy's irregular output landed only a few centimeters from his feet, to the amusement of Robinette, who couldn't resist taunting him with "you're rubbish, go on, piss harder, piss away, you gonna fuck me like that then piss face?" and the two opponents went on pissing, each after his or her own fashion, two whole minutes is a long time to piss, but the two opponents were committed, and although his flow was in no way unorthodox, Casimir High-Life held a steady course, if I'd been in his shoes I'd already have finished pissing and have put my original indivisible element back where it belonged, while this guy had been determinedly flying his flag for over five minutes now, had closed his eyes and tilted his head back, like someone happily humming a requiem for a nun, imperturbable, deaf to all intimidation, to Robinette's many and varied provocations, as gradually she began to step up her urinal output, and suddenly flung at him "come on, crack, you piss pot, crack, you know you will, you don't even know how to piss, crack now, I got liters left in my reservoir, man, I'm warning you now, you watch out now, you better stop pissing if you don't wanna be humiliated in front of all these people, you better stop now, say thank you and goodbye!" she shouted, and the guy just answered "shut up and piss, you old fat hen, the true master does not speak, why should I say 'thank you' and 'goodbye,' not me, not ever, you're the one who's gonna crack, Robinette, and then I'm the one who's gonna fuck you" and he gave a squeeze of his two hairy balls, and the flow of his urine increased several notches, and we all stretched our eyes and stared, because this braggart was now pissing with much more conviction, and we could see that his original indivisible element was twice, three times its original size, and we rubbed our eyes in disbelief, as his pouches swelled up and hung there now like two old gourds filled to the brim with palm wine, and there was jubilation in his pissing, and as he pissed he whistled a snatch from an anthem sung by the scum of Trois-Cents, and after that a baroque concerto, and then a heavy metal Zao number, by which time he had everyone's attention, meanwhile, Robinette was giving it her all, she farted several times, till we had to stick our fingers up our noses and in our ears, it smelled so bad, and ripped through the ear like fireworks at the Feast of the Goat, with an odor of contraband Nigerian camphor, sounding at times like a Mardi Gras trumpet in New Orleans and while we were closely focused on Robinette's elephantine rear quarters, a witness informed us that on the other side, High-Life had turned a decisive corner, a miracle deserving of papal beatification, and we all dashed over to get a closer look, you should never miss a miracle, even if it doesn't take place at Lourdes, you've got to try and witness those moments that people will be talking about centuries from now, better to witness it in person than have some parrot tell you a story of love in the time of cholera, so we all went hurtling over to Casimir High-Life to get a look at his historic miracle, we were all knocked sideways, something unbelievable was happening right before our eyes, you had to be there to believe it, we saw how Casmir High-Life had sketched in the dust with his urine a perfect outline of the map of France, his unremarkable output was now falling in the very heart of the city of Paris, "this is nothing," he said, "I can do China, too, and piss on any given street in the city of Peking" and Robinette, thrown into disarray, turned round and threw us a glance before shouting "hey come back here, you lot, come back, what you all looking at down there then, you all a bunch of homos, then, or what?" but we were all quite captivated by the mysterious boastful contestant and began to applaud him and call him Casimir the Geographer, and he began to rise to the challenge "I'm a marathon man, I am, not a sprinter, I'll screw her, I'll wear her out, just you wait and see" he said, and whistled some more of his Trois-Cent riffraff's anthem, and his baroque concerto and his number by Zao, and we applauded more and more as he added the various regions of France to his map, while alongside his magnificent drawing there was another little drawing, "hey, what's that thing he's drawn next to the map of France, what's that then?" asked one witness, distracted by Casimir High-Life's artistic flair, "that's Corsica, idiot" the artist replied, without interrupting his flow, and we all gave a round of applause for Corsica, and for some the word *Corsica* was a new discovery, and people started mumbling, and arguing, till one guy who was seriously confused asked who the president of Corsica was, what kind of state it was, what its capital city was, whether the president was black or white, and we all shouted him down saying "idiot, imbecile," and by now the two of them had been locked in urinal combat for over ten minutes, and I began to want to have a piss myself, often when one person's pissing it makes you want to do likewise, that's why when you go to the hospital the doctor says to leave the tap running to make you want to go, so anyway on they went, but in the meantime, one of the witnesses, who'd been staring at Robinette's butt the whole time, suddenly whipped his thing out of his pants and began to paw at it feverishly, and we heard a great orgasmic bellow, like that of a decapitated pig at the Feast of the Goat, and the two contestants, still concentrating hard, still focused intently on their task, went on pissing, "hang on, if it's going to be like that I'm stopping, I'm stopping right here and now, I can't work in these kinds of conditions, who do you take me for, eh, I'm serious, I'm stopping now, the show's over" and everyone turned round, and there was Robinette, and she had indeed stopped pissing, claiming that we were putting her off by behaving like infant schoolkids, but at least she had the grace and sportsmanship to go over to Casimir High-Life to finger his thing affectionately and say "you did well, my boy, you win today, you are a true pisser, now let's see if you can come for as long as you can piss, just tell me where and when and I'm all yours" and we all gave her a clap because it was the first time we'd seen her concede like that and indirectly ask for a ceasefire, so Robinette and Casimir High-Life arranged a meeting in a rented room over by the place des Fetes, in Trois-Cents, we weren't too pleased about the private nature of their rendezvous, we would have preferred them to do it there and then, in front of us, and we all went back into the bar feeling a bit disappointed, while Robinette and the victorious Casimir High-Life dived into a taxi and went off to their rented room, and no one knows what happened between the two of them, Casimir High-Life was never seen again, Robinette turns up occasionally, but she won't tell us what happened, my guess is, she probably took a real hammering in bed with Casimir, and wasn't quite up to the mark, otherwise she'd have got us all drunk and given us all the details of her victory over swanky Casimir and his high life

in fact I wouldn't mind screwing Robinette, I haven't had a good screw for a while, beggars can't be choosers, I don't even know if I'd go the whole way with her, women like Robinette must brew up seismic orgasms, you'd have to keep jogging away for hours, whip her up well till she squeals, and one reason I said no to the Stubborn Snail's proposition, much as I'd have liked to take him up on it, was because I didn't want to tread on the Stubborn Snail's toes, it wouldn't have felt right, perched on top of her, imagining the Stubborn Snail himself jigging around on her like an epileptic rabbit, and anyway, what if the boss himself got jealous, and I wouldn't like to mess up my relationship with the Stubborn Snail with that kind of complication, I don't want to fall out with him when he's like a brother to me, and in any case, would Robinette actually let me take a ride on her, a wet dishcloth like me, and there's a big technical problem, I don't think I'm that well endowed, let's be realistic, and considering all the excess baggage she's carrying behind, I'd probably spend the whole day scouring her Nether Regions for her G-spot and only ever get as far as her B-spot, if that, and still have her spots C, D, E, and F to go, so I'd never satisfy her properly, I'd better just forget it, what I really need at this point in the story is a good rest, I don't want to write another word now, not for a while, I just want to drink, do nothing but drink, take huge big gulps of drink, the last I'll ever have, and if my mental arithmetic's up to scratch, I reckon I must have been writing flat out for several weeks now, some people like to make fun of what they call my new occupation, there's even a rumor that I'm working for an exam that'll get me back into teaching, they say that's why I want to stop drinking and stop coming here, but that's nonsense, I'm hardly going to go back into teaching aged sixty-four, am I, in any case, I need a rest, I need to put my pen down, not read back what I've written, and carry on when I'm ready, whenever that may be, but I will carry on, I just don't want to spend all my energy on it, and when I've finished the second half I'll go, go somewhere far, far away, I don't know where, but I'm going, and I don't care what the Stubborn Snail says, I'll be far away by then, far from Credit Gone West

Last Part

today is another day, a grey day, I try not to be sad, and my poor mother, whose spirit still drifts somewhere over the dirty water of the Tchinouka, always used to say you shouldn't let the grey days get you down, perhaps life's waiting for me somewhere, I wish someone would wait for me somewhere, too, and I've been sitting in my corner here since five o'clock this morning, I've got a bit more distance on things now, so I should be able to write about them better, it's four or five days now since I finished the first part of this book, it makes me smile when I read through some of the pages, they go back quite a way now, I wonder whether deep down I should be proud of it, I reread a few lines, but mostly it frustrates me, nothing really fires me up, in fact everything irritates me, it's nobody's fault, I feel weak, my tongue feels mushy, as though I'd eaten a meal of pork and green bananas the previous day, and yet I haven't eaten anything since yesterday, and I've allowed this tide of black thoughts to wash over me, I'm beginning to wonder whether this isn't my will I'm writing, even though I've no right to speak of a will since the day I do pop my clogs I'll have nothing to leave to anyone, all that's just dreaming, but then dreaming's the only thing that helps you keep a grip on this treacherous life, I still have a dream of life, even if my whole life now is lived in a dream, I've never been so clearheaded in all my days

the days pass quickly, though at the time it seems like the opposite, when you're sitting there, waiting for I don't know what, just drinking and drinking, till you can't move because your head's spinning, watching the earth turn around on its own axis and around the sun, even if I've never believed those damn fool theories I used to teach my pupils when I was still a man like other men, you have to be mad to come out with that kind of far-fetched nonsense, because to tell you the truth, when I'm sitting here drinking and relaxing in the doorway of Credit Gone West, it seems impossible to me that the earth I see before me could be around, that it could be spinning away around itself and around the sun as though it had nothing better to do all day than spin around like a paper airplane, go on, somebody, show it to me turning around itself, show it to me turning around the sun, you have to be realistic, surely, let's not allow ourselves to be bamboozled by thinkers who actually shaved themselves with a common flint or a roughly chiseled stone, maybe if they were really modern they used a bit of polished stone, anyway, roughly speaking, if I had to analyze all that in detail, I would say that in the past people divided into two kinds of thinkers, on the one hand the ones who farted in the bath, then went around shouting "I've found it, I've found it" though nobody gave a shit about what they'd found, let them keep their discoveries to themselves, sometimes I've happened to take a dip in the river Tchinouka, which carried off my poor mother, and I never found anything worth talking about there, not every body submerged in that dirty water automatically performs the famous rise to the surface, in fact that's why all the shit from the Trois-Cents is lying on the riverbed, so someone better explain to me why the shit doesn't obey the rule of Archimedes, and then there's the second major category of crank, who were just plain lazy good-for-nothings who sat around the whole time under the nearest apple tree, waiting for apples to drop on their head, something to do with attraction and gravity, I'm opposed to accepted beliefs, as far as I'm concerned the earth is as flat as the Avenue of Independence that runs past the door of Credit Gone West, that's all there is to say about it, I declare the earth is sadly immobile, that it's the sun that goes whizzing around us, because that's what I see as it rises over the roof of my favorite bar, so enough of all this other stuff, and if anyone even tries to persuade me that the earth is round and turns on its own axis and around the sun, I'll chop his head off there and then, even if he does go down shouting "but it does turn" now then, I don't know why, for instance, I haven't yet told the tale of Mouyeké, a guy who used to come here, but doesn't anymore, for reasons which will become apparent, I couldn't not mention this guy, not give him a place in my book, even if he did only pay Credit Gone West a lightning visit, I like people like that myself, you barely glimpse them passing, just a quick walk-on role, a brief silhouette, a shadow flitting by, a bit like that guy they called Hitchcock, who made furtive appearances in his own films, which your average spectator wouldn't even notice, except if he had an expert neighbor whispering in his ear saying "hey asshole, look down there, in the left-hand corner of the screen, see that tubby guy, the one with a double chin, walking across the screen behind the other characters' backs, that's Hitchcock himself" but I have to say that Mouyeké is not of the same stature as our friend Hitchcock, one must be careful not to get carried away with comparisons, Hitchcock was a real life-size character, a talented man, a guy who could make your spine shiver just with a few birds, or a rear window, he could turn you into a psycho with a single characteristic little trick, but Mouyeké's story made me laugh more than shiver, and I don't feel particularly sorry for him either, I've no time for crooks with no talent, people with no personality, so this guy Mouyeké claimed to have been abandoned by his fetish, his amulet, and I use the word *fetish* because Mouyeké himself claims to be descended from great shamans, who can stop the rain from falling, control the heat of the sun, predict the harvest time, read people's minds, and wake up the souls of the dead, just like Christ, who said solemnly to a poor cold corpse "wake up, Lazarus, and walk!" and, while I'm on the subject of resurrection, I should also add that this wretched stiff of a Lazarus was scared shitless of Christ, and in particular of God, who ever since the dawn of time has been perched somewhere up between two cumulonimbus watching us pile up sins, when he could actually help us avoid them with a little intervention from the Holy Spirit, but the Lord our God has perched himself up there to get a panoramic view of all the worst goings-on in the world, and write them down carefully in his little book, ready for the Last Judgment, and when Jesus spoke in the name of his Father who was perched up on high, poor stiff Lazarus woke up with a start and quick as a flash, shivering with fear at the ways of the Lord which are usually impenetrable but which he had attempted to penetrate during his brief stay with the dead, began walking around like a puppet on a string, which is pretty much what Mouyeké went about saying, according to him, the miracles of Christ were as nothing compared to what he could manage himself in the blink of an eye, he'd claim to be able to turn cats' piss into red wine approved by the Societé des Vins du Congo, and he'd do it, that he could give amputees their legs back, and he'd do it, besides, he'd say, the things Christ did that we find so amazing are completely unverifiable, they've been brainwashing us with them for centuries, wowing us like nursery-school kids, apparently people are still arguing about the miracles of Christ today, even the faithful have never seen eye to eye on them, and, this is still according to Mouyeké, we should treat these miracles with caution, whereas his own miracles were all verifiable, without going back to biblical times when those guys only had some rough old stones to set down the Ten Commandments on after God had mumbled them really quietly while hiding himself away as usual between two strata of cumulonimbus, and anyway no one keeps any of God's dozen or so commandments now, people get more of a kick from breaking the rules than from keeping them, in a world in which sex is everywhere, affordable for all, in a world where fidelity has become meaningless, in a world where even monks and cenobites envy the wrongdoers their lecherous ways, in a world ruled by jealousy and envy, in a world where they put people to death by electric chair even though it is written quite plainly in Holy Scripture "Thou shalt not kill," this is how Mouyeké talks, he's always bad-mouthing the Jerusalem Bible, he's not putting God and his lieutenant-colonels on *his* Christmas list, and one day Mouyeké said "my dear friends and fellow negroes, why is it, do you think, that in the Bible all the angels are whites, or something very like it, they might at least put one or two black angels in there, just to butter up the negroes here on earth who refuse to alter their condition on the grounds that the chips were down from the start, on the grounds that the Almighty got their skin color wrong, so there are no black angels in Holy Scripture, and if one or two blacks do ever crop up in it, it's always squeezed in between a couple of satanic verses, often they're devils, or very minor characters, and there were no blacks among Jesus's disciples either, which really is surprising, are we supposed to believe that at the time the Bible soap was running there was no black actor who could play a leading role, I don't think so, but I do understand and forgive the poor whites, you can see why they saddled the negroes with the role of bootblack in daily life here below when from up on high you get the impression negroes don't even exist," that's the kind of thing Mouyéké would say, my own feeling was that for a witch doctor he was just a little bit too familiar with certain things, which, in my opinion carried a whiff of modernity and the kind of discussions held by intellectuals wearing ties and little round glasses, though the long stretch he did in prison wasn't for his ideas, but for cheating and swindling, anyway, after he got out of prison he came bleating his woes to a line of wine bottles here at Credit Gone West, he's a wretched man, a poor specimen, with bulging muscles and bloodshot eyes, a squalid spectacle, they do say cobblers always wear the shabbiest shoes, and to look at him you would well believe it, he should have asked his gris-gris for a new suit, though maybe not an Yves Saint Laurent, like the Printer's, he could have asked them for some shiny shoes like Casimir High-Life's, but the true fact of it was, Mouyéké went around cheating honest folk, innocents who paid him huge sums of money, so on the day of his trial, the old judge who heard his case in the criminal court laid a trap for him, saying "right, I do not intend to waste time on a matter which seems crystal clear to me, just tell us how much money your victims paid you, Mouyéké" and the accused replied "I'm not some small-time witch-doctor, people paid me large sums of money, very large sums indeed, Your Honor, so I must have been worth it, not every witch-doctor gets paid as much as I did" and the judge answered, "what exactly do you mean by 'large sums,' let's have some exact figures, you're not here to take the piss out of people, do you realize I can have you put away this instant if you start playing that little game with me, eh, did you know that?" "yes, Your Honor, I did know that," "well then, give me a straightforward answer, how much money did these honest folk pay you?" and the accused murmured "over one million

Congolese francs per consultation, Your Honor," and the magistrate was speechless for a moment, trying to work out in his head what a huge sum like that meant, and then went on, skeptically, "and what exactly did you have to do for them, it's not everyone has a million Congolese francs in their pocket" "Your Honor, my job was to help them, I made them fetishes, so their businesses would work, I improved their lives, how many people in this country improve other people's lives, d'you think, alas, no one, except me!" and the judge almost laughed in his face, and said "so you were helping other people, do you think I'm stupid, why don't you make some fetishes for yourself, then, so you can get rich, take a look at yourself, you look like someone who spends their life among the dogs and trash cans of Trois-Cents," and Mouyeké said, assuming the serious manner at which criminals are so adept, "Your Honor, fetiches are for helping others, it was what my ancestors did, and that was their legacy to me," "yes, but properly organized charity begins at home, if I was in your shoes I'd start by improving my own life, your own life's not exactly a success," and Mouyeké looked thoughtful and answered "have you ever seen a doctor perform an operation on himself, Your Honor, well, witch doctors are the same, they can't make fetishes for themselves, it just wouldn't work," "well make them for your family then, that way you can cash in on their fortune," and everyone in the room started laughing, and the judge carried on "so you claim to be able to make someone rich, is that right, Mr. Mouyeké?" "yes, Your Honor, that's right, if you come to me for a consultation, I can make you very very rich, and you'll become the top judge in the whole country in less than five minutes and thirty seconds, I promise you, and you won't have to read case files anymore, the truth of each case will dawn with the light of day, and you will make fairer judgments, instead of condemning innocent people like me," "you stick to your own job, my man, I don't need you to help me make fair and impartial judgments, and I'll show you what I mean by that in a minute, because what I like to do with scum like you is have them banged up where they can talk about ancient philosophy with the rats, I don't even have to consult the jury about your case, I'll deal with it personally, because I am the Law" and everyone laughed so hard that the judge almost had to dismiss the court, and the old man in his robe mopped his brow before reading out his expedited decision in a monotonous voice and Mouyéké was sentenced to six months' imprisonment with no chance of parole, a fine of four million Congolese francs, five years' deprivation of civil rights, and everyone applauded, the judge rose and said to the police "take this crook down to where his friends the rats await him!" and so, after six months in prison, he began turning up here, never saying very much, never getting into conversation, but we all knew he was the famous sorcerer crook who wanted to make the judge's fortune in five minutes and thirty seconds flat, and if you're wondering why I've talked about Mouyéké here it's because I came up against a sorcerer myself at one time, and his name was Zero Fault, but anyway, I won't go into that now, I've still got things to write which I fear I'll have forgotten by the morning a few days ago when I walked out of Credit Gone West having resolved to take a break, stop writing, not read back what I'd written for a while, I wandered down toward the Rex District, in the shade of those young girls in flower the Pampers guy was so fond of until he turned into a wreck with a leaking butt, I felt like treating myself for the first time since the good old leap years, I probably had the idea that a quick fuck with the girls would thaw me out a bit, but not a single young girl in flower was prepared to give me even a quick little screw, not even a tiny one, they all said: "you're too old, you can't get it up, you'll be wasting my time, go and try somewhere else, watch some porn, get yourself to an old folks' home, you're a drunken boat, you stink, you talk to yourself in the street, you never shower, you can't stand up straight," and I said "don't care," though at sixty-four I can at least get an erection like a once-glorious racing stallion who's been put out to graze, it's frightening the way people think they can go round underestimating dinosaurs like me, sending them back to Jurassic Park where they came from, never let a donkey kick an old and feeble lion, I don't know who said that, but the girls made it clear, at any rate, that I

was past it, time was up, though I can tell you one thing, time has
nothing to do with it, and I felt belittled, like a piece of wreckage
tossed about on the sea, even though I had ready money in my
pocket that I'd been given in the street, even though I could pay for
my trick in cash, it really makes you wonder in the end if it's money
these girls are after, or just fresh first timers, they should make
their minds up, or all's up with the world, it just goes to show
prostitution's not what it was, these days girls handpick their
clients, soon they'll be demanding to be paid in sterling or Swiss
francs, now in the old days if you wanted some fun you could
spend an excellent evening in exchange for a can of headless
sardines produced in Morocco, but the days of the welfare state are
long since gone, it all comes down to looks these days, appearances
are everything, if you're off to see a tart you need to spray yourself
with perfume by Larazzo, wear a suit by Francesco Smalto, a dress
shirt by Figaret, it's the end of an era, and since that was the way of
it the day I went down to the Rex, and since I'd been turfed out,
like a carpet seller, I gulped back my pride and bid farewell to arms,
"I don't care" I said, and I continued to prowl about the district,
and as there was a power cut all over the city I couldn't see what
was in front of me, there weren't even any cars driving past, then
suddenly, as luck would have it, in one of those tacky little streets
in our district, just at the top of the rue Papa-Bonheur, I saw the
flickering light of a torch, someone was signaling to me from the
other side of the street, I walked toward it and saw that it was a
prostitute nearing retirement age, perhaps with one foot already in
the grave, and I did hesitate for a moment, wondering if the game
was worth the candle, or even the candelabra, but I stopped anyway,
my curiosity aroused, and said abruptly "how much for a trick?"
and an old crone with a face riddled with lines looked me up and
down pityingly and said "where've you been, eh, if you don't know

how much a trick costs around here, it's the same price as usual, nothing's changed, times are hard for everyone" and I felt embarrassed, because I really didn't know the exchange rate for a trick, so I stammered out "it's true, I must admit, I'm not a regular here, I've just come along for something to do, I mean, for some company, it's one hundred and seven years now, since last I saw the moon" and she looked me up and down again pityingly, "come on then, poor old man, don't have a heart attack on me" and she beckoned to me to follow her down a winding, pest-ridden alley leading to the furthest reaches of the district, and went after her, like a desperate shadow because she hadn't said no, so it must be okay, so I could pay according to my mood, and my pleasure and my own rate of exchange, and we walked for about ten minutes, in the blinding absence of light, and for a moment I thought she might be leading me into a trap with her pimps and other accomplices, you can never tell with ladies of the night, but we came to a patch of wasteland and she said "this where we have to do it" and I asked her "is this your place then?" and she said "hey what am I getting into here, have you come to get laid or to hear my life story?" and she pushed open the door of a prehistoric-looking shack built in the corner of the plot, a close-knit family of black cats suddenly scattered, meowing insults at us in slang, and I said to myself "*if someone slits your throat in a dive like this, no one can hear you scream, goodness me, there aren't even any neighbors around, what a fine fucking mess I've got myself into here!*" then the old crone disappeared inside the prehistoric shack, lit a storm lamp and called to me "you coming or not, for fuck's sake, I haven't got all day," those were her words, so I went on into the prehistoric shack, attempting to conceal my misgivings, or should I say my mounting apprehension, and the old crone flung her bag into the far corner of the room, coughed, cleared her throat, before laying herself down on a mattress that smelled of garbage collectors' armpit combined with moldy mushrooms, she lifted her skirt, the kind worn during the German occupation, and said, gnashing her false teeth, "Alice is what they call me, if you want to go to Wonderland, ask me, not one of those young misses still sucking at their mothers' breasts, come on now darling, come close to me," but of course my desire was gone, I just wanted to run for it, get the hell out of there, then I thought maybe that was a bit rude, maybe this was the only trick she'd turn that day, and with a face like the thirteenth fairy at the feast she was unlikely to have clients lining up on the pavement, more likely they'd be crossing the road to avoid her, with her wig covering only about a third of her pate, her overdone make-up, the whiff of granny about her, and her false teeth protruding out of her mouth like a vampire's, and I just wanted out of that prehistoric shack, the smell was so sickening, I'd lost my inspiration, but you should never humiliate a tart, old or not, it always comes back to haunt you one day, you have to remember, tarts, in the end, are human beings like the rest of us, with their pride, and their dignity, and when humiliated, they'll stop at nothing, they turn into furies, I can't think why some people say they've got no brains and only think with the instrument of their trade, it's not true, there's none so sly as a streetwalker, so I decided to stay in the prehistoric shack, and lay down next to old Alice, she smelled of that powder they use to delay the process of decomposition in mortuaries, and the veins in her neck looked like the ribs of an age-old tree, around whose roots hyenas come to piss, and I saw Alice's legs, thin and bowed, "how are you feeling darling?" she said, I didn't reply, she must say that to all her clients, if, that is, she really ever had any, so then Alice with her old and bandy legs removed the string I wore for a belt, and unbuttoned my shabby trousers, and plunged in her hand with its misshapen fingers, and found my somewhat shrunken thing, "I'll take care of it darling, your thing'll stand as straight as it did when you were twenty, I'm used to it, believe me," and she began reminiscing about her days as a young prostitute, when her hands could still drive some miserable, suicidal wretch wild, but her movements were as weak as those of an albatross captured for a joke by the crew of a ship on the high seas, so this old crone, she kneaded, rather than caressed me, and seeing that nothing very concrete was coming of it, she got all agitated, like a mosquito on a swamp, at which I grew more and more ill at ease, I tried to think about the last time I'd done a spot of mountaineering on a mound of Venus, but my recollection was so cloudy, I could only catch the occasional sunny spell, and a sunny spell is not enough to pump back the life into a poor old thing that's running on empty, so then the old crone stood up in a huff and put on the wig that smelled of palm oil, and the skirt from the 1940s, and picked up her bag and said "you're wasting my time, you're just a poor, sad old fool" so then I stood up too, and held out two ten thousand Congolese franc notes and she said "keep your cash, cretin, the humiliation you have just subjected me to does not cost twenty thousand Congolese francs" and Alice practically pushed me out the door yesterday, at four in the morning, I walked along the banks of the river Tchinouka, the water was dirty grey and silent, I counted several animal carcasses, thrown in the water by the bank dwellers, I talked to myself at length, I expect people thought I was mad, a lost soul who saw windmills at every turn and pitched himself into epic conflict with them, "I don't care," I thought to myself, and I went on talking away to myself, and memories began to float back to me, as in a rising of the ashes, and I thought I really hate this river, it's a lagoon of death, the cause of all my grief, the reason for my anger, my irritation, I would love to get back at this river, to tell it to give back my mother's soul, which it swallowed up one day, a day of deepest silence, but I don't want to talk about that chapter of my life just now, I'll come to it a bit later, I don't want to start crying now, and as these were the dog days, it was their season, I saw some dogs mating, I picked up a stone and threw it toward them, and the dogs barked loudly and angrily, then fled, calling me every rude name they could think of, loser, scum, rogue, pathetic biped, and I said "I don't care, I don't understand your canine patois, you go ahead and bark if you're angry, it doesn't bother me," and I pursued my famished road, I thought I must sit down for a moment, then I folded my legs beneath me like a gazelle who kneels down to weep, in fact I was dizzy with hunger, I could feel a hard knot moving about in my stomach, I started to spew up clots of wine, but "I don't care," I said, and while I was at it I had a shit at the foot of a mango tree, though the poor tree had done nothing, and just at that moment some bank dweller who happened to be passing said "poor bugger, sad old fuck of yesteryear, polluter of public spaces, shitting at the foot of a tree at your age, have you got no shame?" and I said out loud "I don't care, the sad old fuck of yesteryear says fuck off yourself!" and the bank dweller was furious and added "don't you speak to me like that you old pisshead, fuck off and die then, shithead!" so I said again, out loud, "I don't care, you'll die before I do, the cemeteries round here are stuffed full of young idiots like you!" and the bank dweller said threateningly "pick up your shit or I'll throw you in the river," and he was serious about it, and I didn't want to meet my death by drowning over some silly shit at the foot of a mango tree, and as it was actually my shit I began to pick it up, and the bank dweller said "what are you doing, old man, you can't go picking up your own poop with your bare hands, you should do it with the end of a stick, for Christ's sake" but I ignored him, because actually there's nothing sickening about picking up your own shit, it's other people's shit that's revolting, so I plunged my hands into my excrement, and the bank dweller threw up and scarpered, revolted by this scatological scene, and I began to laugh and laugh and laugh

my wanderings brought me at the stroke of five in the morning to Credit Gone West, I was still haunted by the image of Alice's thin, bandy legs, and of her prehistoric shack, and then I recalled the scene with me picking up the shit with my bare hands instead of using the end of a stick, so that when I got here at five in the morning I still stank of shit, and I dozed for a while on a stool at the bar and was woken up by the smell of coffee Dengaki had made for me, he said it was from the boss, and I glanced upstairs and there was still a light on in the Stubborn Snail's room, and I accepted the coffee, though they don't serve coffee here, the boss must have made it himself upstairs and had it sent down, I started on a bottle of red, it was the beginning of a new day, but a day unlike any other, I said to myself it's around one or two in the afternoon when I notice that never-ending pain in the neck, the Printer, is back at Credit Gone West, I don't know why I call him a pain in the neck, since up till now he'd made a fairly favorable impression, but only fools never change their minds, so anyway, the Printer had finished his long walk over on the Côte Sauvage and was happy as anything, seemed so excited you'd think they'd just elected him president of Senegal, I've never seen him on such good form, so what's going on, ah, now I see, that's what it was, now I see why he's in such a good mood, I understand now, it's because he's got hold of a copy of *Paris Match* and he's proud of it, he's showing off, he's ecstatic, and he's trying to explain to everyone else about these two French artists who are having a hard time because they're a famous couple, it seems, and he says it's there in black-and-white in the magazine, he tells us how these two artists are being pestered by the kind of people who hide out in the shrubbery with their cameras and hope to catch a glimpse of the tits and asses of famous divas, and some people are listening to the Printer, some people are actually listening, as you might listen to the guru who's having sex with the wife of the

Pampers guy, and since there's no stopping him once he's started he's now telling everyone yet again about his French experience, how he "did" France, and how white Céline was the author of his decline, his Dark Empire, he's not mad, he tells them, far from it, but Céline actually slept with his Caribbean son, he tells them all about that, and people look at him pityingly, and one guy actually tells him straight out he should have married an African woman in France, not a white woman, and things would have been less complicated and they could have sorted it all out back home with a few Rwandan machetes, but the Printer replies that African women in France are a tight-assed lot, stuck-up, affected, unreliable, he can't stand all that, they think an awful lot of themselves, those girls do, they want you to grovel at their feet, what's more, says the Printer, they're all materialistic, they check out your car, your house, your bank account, your shares on the stock market, you have to pay for their ridiculous hairdos that cost a fortune, you have to pay the rent for their box rooms in the Sixteenth Arrondissement, because that's the only arrondissement in Paris these little madams will live in, even if they have to shack up in cellars somewhere, you end up paying for this, that, and the next thing, that's why they hang out on street corners, why they live off benefits, and grow old in the pursuit of their vanity, that's why they sleep with white men three times their age, that's why they sometimes fall into prostitution, because it's easier to turn your body into a piece of merchandise than your brain into an instrument of reflection, and people started laughing, and the Printer was pleased with his effect on his audience, "listen, I'm no racist," he said, and went on to issue a whole string of extremely dubious prejudices, slagging off the black girls in Paris, calling them every name under the sun, and the Congolese girls, by the way, he said, were not even worth mentioning, they were way dependent, and like to think they're intellectuals, there is no worse than the Cameroonians who are so materialistic and greedy that they are called the Came*ruin*ians, he said the Nigerian girls spend the whole time fighting each other for a place on the rue Saint-Denis, he says the Gabonese are a whole different story, they're just crab ugly, the Ivory Coast girls are incredible, slags and slappers who go round wiggling their asses all day, and the people at Credit Gone West think it's hilarious and the Printer reminds them once again that of course he doesn't belong here in this bar, and the others listen to him respectfully, they agree with him, and they pass around *Paris Match*, and the Printer reminds them that he used to be in charge of a team, with real whites in it, not the whites you see here, chewing manioc and drinking Beninese beer, but real French whites, and he stresses that they were the people who printed *Paris Match*, and I thought to myself, this guy's a real weirdo, it's about time he changed the record

so when he's quit playing to the gallery, the Printer comes over to me and says "I don't know if anyone's told you this, my friend, but you stink of shit, you can smell it a mile off, have you crapped in your pants, or what, you ought to go and take a shower, look, you're even attracting the flies," and I don't reply, I'm not going to tell him someone told me to pick up my own shit which I'd dumped at the foot of a mango tree, no way, and the Printer adds "okay, it's your shit, nothing to do with me, what I really wanted to tell you was, I have here, in my hands, the latest copy of *Paris Match*, I bought it this morning, as I was taking my usual stroll down to the Côte Sauvage, go on, take a look, it's got some ass in it, and it's free," so out of politeness I take the magazine and flick through it, and I come across a guy called Joseph, a black painter, who's sick with something, terribly thin, in the picture he's wearing an army-surplus shirt and he's sitting with his eyes shut in a room in a hospital with all his canvases and work things next to him, he looks really eaten up by his illness, and at his bedside there's even a book about the painter Picasso, and on top of this book the sick man's laid out his paintbrushes, and I discover that no one knows the painter's real name, or who he is, that he's a Parisian street painter, a painter from the district they call the Marais, but most of all I'm shocked to read that he's just died of cancer, and the article goes on to explain how he was hospitalized two months ago, and put on the respiratory ward at St. Antoine Hospital, living from one bout of chemotherapy to the next, homeless, living on the streets, drinking bottle after bottle of whiskey, smoking endless packs of cigarettes, and I feel a kind of tenderness for this character, he even looks a bit like me, and the journalist in *Paris Match*, whose name was Pepita Dupont, went and interviewed this black van Gogh just eight days before he died, and it turns out that the negro in question was a real walking library, he's read his Arthur Rimbaud and his Benjamin Constant and his Baudelaire and above all his Chateaubriand, in particular the *Mémoires d'outre-tombe*, he talks like a book himself, he finds just the right expression, the journalist is amazed, he also talks about famous painters whose names I've never heard before, because I don't know anything about painting, and he mentions painters called William Blake, Francis Bacon, Robert Rauschenberg, James Ensor, and lots more and the journalist says that this painter could easily have vanished without trace, someone just happened to discover him by chance and befriended him, and this savior is a lawyer who found Joseph lying on the pavement with his canvases, the lawyer was just moving into a new building, where the black van Gogh had lain down for the night, the lawyer almost tripped over him as he lay sleeping on his masterworks, and they got into conversation, and the lawyer fell in love with this man's original art, and he examined the paintings closely, and bought several of them, and became a great friend of the black van Gogh and every day they talked together, and the lawyer couldn't get over the fact that this original art had gone unnoticed all this time, but he knew that true art, the real kind, always meets with indifference, genius is often unacknowledged in its own time, victim of a confederacy of dunces, and the lawyer realized that what he had discovered here was an *artiste maudit*, so he decided he would help him, and bring him to the notice of the art scene, make him famous throughout Paris, in the closed and fusty world of art, and he introduced him to a decent guy who runs the Dubuffet Foundation, and this guy was bowled over too, and said that the black van Gogh was a genius, beyond all doubt, so the lawyer and the guy from the Dubuffet Foundation decided to wave a magic wand over Joseph's life, but unfortunately Joseph departed this life rather soon after that, and he went instead to practice his art alongside his illustrious masters, the Picassos, the Rauschenbergs, and all the rest, everyone knows that truly great artists attain glory after their deaths, however hard the living hustle for recognition and acclaim, that's only success, not glory, and success is to glory as a shooting star is to a sun, and when the sun sets in one place, it rises somewhere else, to bring light to lands anew, to send forth new rays of glory, and even the true van Gogh, it seems, sold only one painting in his lifetime, and since Joseph's death, according to *Paris Match*, his stock rises every day, collectors call from all over the world, trying to get their hands on his paintings, the ones he did on old bits of cardboard, with inscriptions from *The Count of Monte Cristo*, apparently the black van Gogh knew whole passages of Alexandre Dumas's novel by heart, and of Chateaubriand, Joseph says he's awesome, and adds "he writes not with a pen but with a whip, he shouts at you, I couldn't put *Atala* down, I wept when I found out afterwards that Chateaubriand's father was a slave trader, he never mentions it in his *Memoirs*," and when I read that in *Paris Match*, the thing that struck me most was his courage in the face of the illness which would eventually kill him, he's basically saying "this illness is devouring my life, and I can only deal with it by painting, I'm using my paintbrush to sweep away this fucking cancer" and while I'm trying to finish reading this moving article on Joseph the black van Gogh, the Printer starts to shake me and threaten me and even tries to snatch the magazine away "for fuck's sake Broken Glass, get a grip, why are you wasting your time on the dead, he's nothing, that guy, I don't even want to see his photo, he's a loser, a piece of garbage, come on, turn the page," so I skip a few pages and he shouts "slow down, slow down, you just missed the page with the pussy on it, it's on page thirteen" and I turn back to page thirteen, and there is actually a bare piece of ass on it, but quite honestly it's a bit blurred round the edges, and I'm feeling really fed up, and I say "how do I know that picture's not faked, I can't make much out, it could be anybody's ass" and the Printer gives an angry shout, he can't bear it if anyone contradicts him on this subject, and he yells at me "what you saying there, Broken Glass, what you saying, you mad or what, a guy like you, over sixty, a wise man like you, how can you say something so stupid, eh, you saying this photo's not for real, that what you mean, eh, you think a magazine like *Paris Match* is going to print photos that aren't even true, can't you see it's in color, can't you see these are professional photographers risking their lives, these are serious journalists writing this stuff, can't you see that pussy is real pussy, the stuff your average Frenchman in his Basque beret dreams of, shit man, you must be blind" and I mumble, as though fearful of his reaction, "yeah, but you shouldn't believe everything you read in some trashy magazine, those guys can sell you anything as long as there are people who'll buy it" and then he gets really mad and says "listen to me, Broken Glass, first thing, this is not a trashy magazine, this is a serious publication, reinforced concrete, man, I can swear to that, because we actually printed it in France, and I can tell you everything that's in it is true, and that's why everyone buys it, politicians, superstars, big businessmen, famous actors, they all fall over each other to get themselves and their families into it, in front of their houses, with their dogs and their cats and their horses, and I'll tell you this too, when the politicians over there get into trouble with the law, or for sleaze, or faked accounts, or allocation of government contracts, illicit use of influence, all that kind of stuff, they always try to get themselves photographed in *Paris Match*, to show what decent guys they are and anyone trying to make trouble for them must just be jealous, or a political opponent, trying to stop them standing in the next elections, you see what I mean, take a look at page twenty-seven, there's a politician there, he's totally corrupt, he's got all sorts of dirty baggage, he's involved in some of the worst scandals in the whole of France, but there he is, in *Paris Match*, and it looks good, let me tell you," and I'm trying to concentrate on page thirteen, with the blurred pussy, "I'm sorry, but I still think it's not a genuine photo, you can tell just by looking at it" and he snatches the magazine out of my hands, he's really cross now, he feels personally affronted, and he walks away muttering nastily "sad old fuck of yesteryear, I thought you were okay till now, but I think old age must be rotting your brain, and you stink of shit, go and have a wash" and he spits on the ground and then says "we just don't share the same values, you and I, you're from different eras, you're yesterday's man, I don't even know what you're doing here, I never want to speak to you again, it's over, I'm not coming near you, shit, it's like you're forgetting I've done France, no one here but me's seen snow, no one here's seen the Champs-Elysées or the Arc de Triomphe" and with this he walks off, flustered and furious, and I say darkly to myself "I just don't give a shit, this old man of yesteryear says you go fuck yourself" and he goes and sits with a group of blind-drunks who are talking about the match between the formidable Southern Sharks and the tenacious Northern Reptiles, it seems the Northern Reptiles won a clear 2-0 victory, but it also seems that in the first leg the Southern Sharks won with the same score, so there should be another match in two weeks' time, according to these idiots sitting round chewing the cud like a band of impotents with nothing to do, and the Printer interrupts their sporting banter saying "hey, you guys, what's going on here, what is this place, you all going mad, or what, let's just be serious for a moment, fuck it, there's lots of things more important than these barbaric games of soccer" and he passes around his magazine, which some people like but not the ones who are crazy about soccer

I stand up to stretch my legs and get something to eat, and I think what a strange day this is, starting at five in the morning with picking up the shit, not a good sign, and now everyone seems on edge, I think this is my last day in this place, even if I don't really believe it, I still think it's my last day here, you have to know when to draw the line, that's what I tell myself, as I leave the bar, taking my lost illusions with me, and cross the Avenue of Independence, there's Mama Mfoa selling meat kebabs opposite Credit Gone West, she's bald and sometimes will sing for us, that's why we affectionately call her the bald soprano, she sells grilled sole, TV chicken, and bicycle chicken, I don't like the TV chicken because it's made in the microwave, so I usually have the bicycle chicken, which is cooked on a barbecue, and some people say unkindly that our bald soprano puts fetishes in the food, that's why she always has customers even when times are hard, and they also say her delicious kebabs are just made of pieces of local dog or cat meat, but that wouldn't make me want to throw up anyway, I don't believe nonsense like that, and if her meat really is local dog or cat meat one can only say that the local dogs or cats are very tasty, and we've all eaten local dog or cat meat before now, it's true that her little stall is always busy, I think that's because the bald soprano is kind, it's because she's a real mother hen, she always has a kind word for each of us, and she doesn't really mind whether you pay her, you have to almost beg her to get her to take the money, she always says "don't worry, papa, you just pay me when you can" but we shouldn't accept her generosity because she has to pay her rent and feed her family, so when you pay her she piles your plate higher than any other food seller in the district, some people even choose their chunks of meat from the pot, and she gives us manioc for free, that's her way of attracting customers from Trois-Cents, and that's why we like her, all the rest is literature, bad Black-African literature, the kind you find on the banks of the Seine, it's just babble, people talk but they still eat their local dog or cat kebabs, which is incredible, and they even say that the oil she uses for frying is a mixture of her spittle and piss, and that's why her kebabs taste like those fish balls you get in Japanese cooking, but it's just a windup, I don't believe it, Mama Mfoa is an honest citizen, like the Stubborn Snail is, a person who will have nothing to reproach herself for on the Day of Judgment, she's already got a seat with her name and number on in paradise

so our dear bald soprano sees me arrive at her little stall and she smiles and says "so what would you like to eat today, papa Broken Glass, you don't look well" she calls all the Credit Gone West customers *papa*, it's her way of showing her affection, and I tell her to give me a bicycle chicken with lots of chili, and I tell her to give me some manioc, I take it all, I pay, she says "I really think you should stop drinking, papa, that Sovinco red wine is no good," and I say, "I'm stopping today, this is my last day, my last glasses of wine, I swear," and she smiles and continues "I mean it, Broken Glass, it's not good to drink, look how much weight you've lost, you used to be a fine-looking man, you're wasting away, you should give up the bottle," and I promise her again that I'll give up my bottle worship and my red wine tonight at midnight, "I don't believe you, what will you drink if you give up" she asks, straight out, and I tell her I'll drink still water, lots of still water, and she shakes her head, she doesn't believe me, and says "I'll believe that when I see it, and another thing, papa, I suggest you take a shower, I don't know if you sat in some shit, but it smells really bad," and I think, it must be that smell of shit still hanging around, I watch her turn over the TV chicken in the microwave, and plunge the carp into the boiling oil, and wipe her face with the back of her hand, her sweat is even running down into the pot, but who cares, that's what gives her food its flavor, I say to myself, this woman is truly an exceptional person, she sits there surrounded by her cooking utensils, committed to her work, and I wonder if she really does that to earn her nightly crust, perhaps she does it for the love of her fellow man, and while I'm thinking about that, she says again "it's not good to drink, papa, you ought to stop, I know people who've ended up in the Etatolo Cemetery thanks to the bottle, I can tell you, a drunk's corpse is not a pretty sight, the skin's strange, red as wine, it's awful, I don't want your corpse to look like that the day you die, you know what I mean" and she tells me about a guy called Demoukoussé, one of God's own drinkers, his skin turned red, it had great big mushrooms growing on it, according to Mama Mfoa, Demoukoussé had never drunk a drop of water, he died one day in a bush in the Fouks District, holding his glass bottle, they buried him with a crate of wine, as requested in his will, which was duly respected, but I didn't know the guy, he never came to Credit Gone West, so that's why there's no point dwelling on him, it would just be useless compilation, and Mama Mfoa notices that I fail to respond to her story about Demoukoussé, and she says "papa, I'm sorry, I hope you're not annoyed, I only said that because I care about you, I wouldn't have said it if I didn't, believe me, papa, I don't want you to die like Demoukoussé, you deserve better," and at last she serves me, and I take my bicycle chicken, I sniff it, it's well cooked, the onion makes me sneeze, she looks at me and murmurs gently, "bon appétit, little papa," and I cross back over the Avenue of Independence and go and eat in my usual corner in fact when the boss of Credit Gone West asks "how are things with you, Broken Glass?" I really don't know what to say, he already knows everything about me, he knows why I spend all my time here, he knows it's because of Angelica, he saw Angelica come and chase me out of here a few years ago, before he even finished putting the roof on, and what else can I tell him, I've nothing new to add, but it's true that I'm writing in this notebook, I don't know who else will read it, and whoever the curious reader may be, he'll know nothing about all that unless he's part of our inner circle and he'll be wondering what could have happened to me, he'll be saying "it's all very well to talk about other people, it's all very well sitting eating your bicycle chicken in a corner, that's all fine, but what happened to you, Broken Glass, tell me about yourself, tell me everything, don't tiptoe around, tell us your tale," so I really must talk about myself too, the curious reader needs to know something about how I came to fall so low without a parachute, he needs to know why I now spend my time here, so it's not just a blank in his mind, I keep telling him over and over I'm a fossil in this place, so here we go, to start with, I need to make clear that Angelica is the first name of my ex-wife, but whenever I mention her I call her Diabolica, and throughout this notebook I'm going to call her Diabolica, yes, that's what I'll call her, there's nothing angelic about her, quite the opposite, angels, even drunken ones, don't act like that, Diabolica spent over fifteen years by my side, and through all those years she nurtured the hope that she would one day convince me that the arch of her back was more exciting than that of a bottle of red wine, while I spent fifteen years trying to convince her of the opposite, because I can drink from a bottle anytime, anyhow, anywhere, it depends on me, and what I want and what time I arrive at Credit Gone West, but with Diabolica I never felt I was in the presence of a woman

I know my chicken's going to go cold, I know I should eat, but I must just say a few words about my life, to do with Diabolica, so, in the beginning, she used to come and haul me out of the bar and take me home, but the minute she'd gone to bed I'd come back again, and the next day she'd start sniveling and saying we no longer spent any time together, our life together was becoming unbearable, and I always came home at first crow of the cock who sits in the top of the mango tree on our compound, and on some occasions I actually slept at the foot of the mango tree, to be woken by the warm, diarrheal droppings of the cock who sits in its branches to announce the dawning of a new day, and so when Diabolica opened the door in the morning she would find me outside in a pool of my own urine, my blackish, liquid excrement, and would dissolve into tears, call the neighbors in the hope of shaming me into changing my ways, and I told the neighbors to bugger off, I wanted nothing to do with them, and asserted my right to privacy, and one of these neighbors, the one I hated most, said "when someone disturbs everyone around him like that, he forfeits his right to privacy, one man's freedom ends where the next man's begins" he liked to think of himself as some kind of Enlightenment philosopher, we had even almost come to blows because he was always trying to prove to me that he had more general culture than me, well, be that as it may, one day, at the end of the small hours, Diabolica said loud and clear that enough was enough, there was a limit to her patience, she was not going to spend her entire life looking after a walking corpse like me I caused her nothing but misery, and she also said I was nothing but a merchant of tears, I was trampling on the tapestry of her present time and therefore it was clear, I must make my choice, once and for all, I must choose between her and alcohol, a most Cornelian dilemma, so I said yes to alcohol, and she began weeping in the evenings, when I didn't come home or I slept beneath the mango tree in our compound, and she discussed it with our neighbor, the Enlightenment philosopher, who said it was as if I were dead, as if I were a phantom of the opera, as if I were the serial killer with a stick and Diabolica went along with this bargain-basement philosophizing, and added that she would have preferred me to die a quick and sudden death, rather than this death on credit, which was far harder for her, she would have preferred me to die, so that she could at last recover some of her freedom, she said she was sick of the way local people looked at her, people were laughing at her, even the dogs barked as she went by, though it wasn't her who drank, she swore that if it continued she would throw herself into the river Tchinouka, and I tried to comfort her, I found some cast-iron arguments, for example, I said, seriously and solemnly, that it was better to drink than to smoke but she immediately countered by saying that drinking and smoking were tobacco from the same pipe, water from the same tap, therefore you shouldn't drink, and therefore you shouldn't smoke, otherwise you'd be off to the next world in an open coffin, and again I laughed, I couldn't see I was doing any harm by drinking, and besides, I'd never hit Diabolica, she was the one who pushed me about, and yelled at me when she was angry, that's what used to happen, and yet I was, and remain, a passive, not an aggressive drinker, she knew perfectly well that I understood what was meant by nonviolence, that my favorite poster was the one that shows King looking at the picture of Ghandi, there's no better proof than that that I'm a supporter of nonviolence, you won't find me attacking the second sex, why would I want to do that, and then I asked her "have I ever beaten you, have I ever attacked someone in the street, has anyone ever come round here complaining about me, never, and I'm not going to suddenly start hitting people tomorrow, you can call me anything, home bird or fly-by-night, dismiss me as an approximate man, demean me in front of others, I don't give a damn, each of us arrives on this earth with his own burden to bear, you can't push me down any lower than that, I know what I'm doing even if I drink, go ahead and make a black-and-white song and dance about it, I don't care," that's what I said every time, I swear on the grave of my mother who drowned in the dirty water of the Tchinouka

and Diabolica would explain to anyone who cared to listen that I was possessed, bewitched by the devil, that I was captive to a tenacious creature with a long pointed tail, a creature who charmed me with eyes like volcanoes, and she explained that I was the plaything of this demon, that the words of my lips were the words of Satan, explaining the earth to the good Lord, and since I know nothing about that kind of thing, and believed only the evidence of my own eyes, one day she pronounced, urbi et orbi, that she would give me one last chance, that I had to take it, there would be no further reprieves or probation, she said "drinking's all very well, but you shouldn't pollute the lives of those who don't, what's going on here, d'you think I'm going to spend my whole life like this," in fact, she added, alcohol did more damage to those who don't drink than to those who do, and when I drank it was as though she drank, so she was twice as drunk as I was, in fact it was our philosopher neighbor who had doused her in all these crazy ideas, which she'd then taken seriously, and the neighbor said that Diabolica was a "rebound victim," at which point the neighbor started to get seriously on my nerves, and I laughed at the idea of this kind of fancy thinking coming from someone who hadn't even studied medicine in Paris, what's more, there are some doctors who smoke like firefighters, which is a bit rich, so how could what I drink end up in her stomach, and make her drunk, as if she were the one who'd been drinking, God's no fool, after all, each of us is separately made, there isn't some invisible link running from one person's stomach to the next, each of us swallows his own pint, into his own small intestine, his own pancreas, my bile is my bile, and his bile is his, that's all there is to it, and that's what I told Diabolica and our neighbor, the Enlightenment philosopher, but it was the last chance my wife was giving me, I was waiting to see what she'd do when I refused to yield to her demands, and she said "I'm not kidding when I say this is the last chance I'm giving you, it'll end badly, this business, you mark my words," and I just laughed and said "promises, promises," and went on boozing, tipping back the red wine, decapitating, eviscerating those poor bottles of Sovinco, forgetting I'd ever been married, that Diabolica was my wife, and one day some neighbors who had converted to Islam came to drag me out of Credit Gone West to tell me my wife had been bitten by a snake, I told them I wasn't married and that no black child was interested, these days, in the story of the visiting snake, and I heard the Muslim neighbors murmuring that it would have been better if Allah had removed me from this life, that I was no longer worthy of it, they said I was reduced to a mere shadow, a specter without a grave, now those Muslim neighbors were right, my wife had actually been bitten by one of those black snakes that swarm around Trois-Cents, as though they had been driven out of the wooded savanna, even the snakes had joined the rural exodus, and had all made a beeline for Diabolica, but I didn't really give a fuck, my thoughts were elsewhere, and perhaps it was the incident of the black snake which screwed everything up and pushed Diabolica to make a move

and so, one hot, sunny day, my wife's family turned up at our house, she held a little ethnic council of war, with me as the topic of their byzantine discussion, the one and only Broken Glass, they discussed me from every angle, and issued an edict, and condemned me in absentia because I didn't turn up at their tribunal, it was as though I'd sensed in advance that they had set a trap for me, I'd followed my instincts and left the house the previous day, and that's how I narrowly escaped the clutches of these reactionaries, these champions of the rights of man, these killjoys, sons of chaos, sons of hatred, but I reckoned without the vigilance and rancor of Diabolica, who knew just where to find me, and she dragged the family welcoming committee out into the street, down the Avenue of Independence, even the people in the street thought they must be part of the strike by the *battú*, the poor people of Trois-Cents, because it has to be said, my ex-parents-in-law are a band of vagrants and vagabonds, real hillbillies, their clothes all grubby and worn, which is not surprising, they're poor up-country mujiks, who think only of tilling the land or watching out for the rainy season, and such is their greed, they'd sell a dead man's soul to the first bidder, they don't know how to behave, they've never learned to eat at the table, or use a fork, or a spoon, or a table knife, they spend their whole low-down existence hunting ground squirrels, fishing for catfish, and you can't begin to talk about culture with them, because, as the singer with a mustache says, their brains are scarcely bigger than thimbles, so, these cavemen came to drag me away from my lofty preoccupations at Credit Gone West, and read out the conviction reached in my absence, they had decided to take me to a healer, a witch doctor, or rather, a sorcerer named Zero Fault, to get him to drive out the tenacious devil dwelling within me, and break me of the habit of worshipping under the sun of Satan, and we had to go to his place, to the house of that idiot they called Zero Fault, but I wasn't afraid, I really wanted to piss them off, so I said "just leave me alone, I'm not bothering anyone, just sitting there drinking my own drink, why is everyone against me, I don't want to go to see Zero Fault" and all the good people in my wife's family said in chorus "you have to come with us, Broken Glass, you've got no choice, we're taking you there, even if we have to do it in a wheelbarrow," and I replied, howling like a hyena caught in a wolf trap, "no, no, no I'd rather die than come with you to Zero Fault's," and since there were quite a few of them, they caught hold of me, jostled me, threatened me, pinned me down, and I was shouting, "shame on you, ye of little faith, you can't do anything to me, who ever heard of mending a Broken Glass" and they jammed me into a ridiculous wheelbarrow and the whole district was laughing at this outrageous scene, because they were treating me like a sack of cement, and I was insulting Zero Fault all the way along my way of the cross while my wife was still going on about the black snake who'd bitten her and I asked her which black snake that was, "the snake of Satan, you made it come, I've never been bitten by a black snake in my life" she cried, and I went on saying "black snake, really black snake, and how come you saw it in the night if it was black?" and she almost tipped up the wheelbarrow, but her aunt calmed her down, saying "take it easy, niece, Zero Fault will take care of him in a little while, we'll soon see whether the devil and the good Lord can sup together without either one using a long spoon"

they dragged me inside Zero Fault's house, I was humming to myself, I forget what, but who knows why the caged bird sings, I was probably humming the Song of Solomon, the wheelbarrow was jolting about, almost tipping over, miraculously I didn't fall out, and people were taking it in turns to push it, they were really pissed with me because I was burping all the time and threatening to pee and shit, and eventually we arrived at the top of a hill, before Zero Fault's old shack, on the opposite bank of the river Tchinouka, and the sorcerer, who had seen us coming from a distance, said "miscreants, take off your shitty shoes, rid yourselves of evil thoughts, this is my home, the kingdom of our ancestors" and the whole cortege promptly complied, as though the words came from the Holy Spirit incarnate, my wife took off my little shoes *manu militari*, and they threw my little shoes into a corner, I said to my wife "don't forget my little shoes" and they gave gifts to Zero Fault, who was cooing thanks in C major, though they came out sharp, the guy was so louche, and I saw at once that Zero Fault was very far from being a real healer, he was like the one who'd wanted to make the judge rich, the one I mentioned at the start of this second section, whose name was Mouyeké, and Zero Fault was nothing like a real sorcerer either, because I do actually know how to recognize a real sorcerer, and he wasn't even a gentleman crook, he was the Confidence Man, and I challenged him, I said to Confidence Man, "if you're a real healer, if you really are genuine, as you say, tell me my birth date and birthplace, in front of all these witnesses, tell me about my family tree, give us some proof of your esoteric knowledge" and my parents-in-law, these mujiks who could sell a dead man's soul, these *battú*, these men and women peasants all looked at me in horror and shouted at me, baying for my blood, and told me to stop playing the fool or divine retribution would come down upon me while Zero Fault was getting in touch with the ancestors, they pushed me up against the wall and, cheeky as ever, I went on "yeah, 'cause the real sorcerers from Loubloulou, my native village, can tell you where and when you were born, you can't do that, I know you can't, and you know you can't," the atmosphere was starting to get really strained, and my wife said to me "Broken Glass, could you just zip your big mouth a minute and let Zero Fault do his work," but I didn't stop, I banged another nail into my own coffin by saying to the people present "that guy is a first-rate imposter, he's not a real sorcerer, he's not a real healer, he just wants to fleece you, like all the confidence men in this country want to fleece honorable citizens, he's the devil, not me, let me tell you, vade retro me, Satana," my wife's family all began shouting insults at me, while I went on reciting my heresies and my wife cried "shut up now Broken Glass, why are you talking like that to a man feared by the entire district, are you mad or what" and I laughed, and gave the con man the finger, I spat on the ground, and my father-in-law said "I must say, your husband is no longer the man I knew" and then my mother-in-law said "by God's grace may our ancestors forgive us for the ravings of my son-in-law, I never knew Satan could put such blasphemy in the mouth of one of God's creatures," and the brother-in-law said "he's no creature of God, he's the Antichrist in person" and all the mujiks and the ostrogoths and peasant men and peasant women began saying much the same thing, and my wife spoke up again, because she wanted to set the record straight, and she said "Broken Glass, I demand that you apologize this instant to Zero Fault and to the ancestors, who look down upon us as we speak, it's your fault they're not getting through" and Zero Fault, who was pretending to be meditating, finally spoke, with a sigh, saying "madame, I thank you for these words of wisdom, but you must understand that the devil is inside your husband's body, those are the words of the demon, I promise you that we will drive out the devil from his body, believe me, I'm not called Zero Fault for nothing, and as you all know, I've fought much greater spirits than that" and I carried on ranting, shouting "stop talking rubbish, you low-down liar, you low-down criminal, low-down dream seller, low-down man with seven names or so, low-down bully boy, low-down charlatan, low-down conjuror without talent, low-down profiteer, low-down capitalist, vade retro me, Satana," I said all that and Zero Fault suddenly became angry and lost control and showed his yellowest smile and bared his old charred stumps, which was just what I was hoping for, I wanted him to lose his temper, and he said "call me a capitalist, do you, you dare to call me a capitalist, am I a capitalist, d'you think, you say those blasphemous words once more in front of the ancestors and I'll smash your face in," that's what he was shouting, and I just carried on, I said "yeah, you're a low-down capitalist, a real low-down capitalist, you're into the exploitation of your fellow man, vade retro me, Satana" and he got angrier still and said to my wife "listen madame, I can't work like this, your husband does not respect me, he doesn't respect the ancestors, he dares to call me a capitalist, I can go along with a devil who tells me vade retro me, Satana, but I won't be called a capitalist, do I go round exploiting the poor, d'you think, do I love profit, d'you think, am I into the exploitation of my fellow man, d'you think, I'm Zero Fault himself, I am, you can ask anyone, they'll tell you I've restored the eyes of the blind, the legs of the lame, the voices of the dumb and the ovaries of sterile women, the erections of men who couldn't get it up, even in the morning, when his piss usually makes any man's thing stand up, and did you know, by the way, that I helped the mayor of this town get reelected for life, not to mention the students and their exam results, the administrative posts I've secured for people who never even went to school, or the way I got the wife of the prefect of the region to go back to her husband, I'm not called Zero Fault for nothing, did you know that when the Adolphe-Cisse Hospital abandons all hope, I'm the one who goes in to help the poor cripples, so when I come across imbeciles like this one, like your husband here, trying to tarnish my legendary reputation, and desecrate the masks of the ancestors here on my wall, I tell myself this world is seriously screwed, that through him the Antichrist is with us here below, this man's place is in the asylum, so would you kindly take that piece of rubbish home with you, hell, what's going on here, get out, I said, I refuse to help this man, he has no respect for me, get out of this holy place before I put a curse on you," and I began laughing again like a coyote belting out some Mississippi gospel, or a mountain wolf having a shot at a baroque concerto, and I said to my wife "don't forget my little shoes" and my wife's family put me back in the wheelbarrow because they were afraid Zero Fault would put a curse on them, because they were afraid that the curse might mean the family offspring would have snouts or pigs' tails or trotters, so that's how they brought me home again and how they came to think of me as an idiot, but happily I managed to escape the criminal clutches of Zero Fault, vade retro me, Satana

my sufferings were far from over though, because Diabolica was still not happy, so she decided to wean me, imposing a ban on hanky-panky for the next few days, weeks, and months, now I like a bit of that when I've had a drink, it's good when you've a had a drink, you feel like you're flying, like you're gaining altitude, but Diabolica wanted nothing to do with me, apparently I stank, I was no longer the same man, sometimes I was rather like Satan, and yet I didn't want to rape her, no way, that's not the kind of thing I'd do, so I haven't got my leg over ever since then, and a bit later on, when things were getting worse by the day, Diabolica sat me down at the foot of the mango tree on our compound, she had something important to say to me, but I didn't want to hear, I said "let me be, I haven't got my leg over for longer than I can remember, I'm not going to talk unless I get my leg over" and she looked at me pityingly, she started talking in this sad sort of voice, she almost had me crying, saying how I was known to everyone in the district now as a drunk, where I'd once been an excellent primary-school teacher at Trois-Martyrs, she said I no longer read my Frédéric Dard (alias San-Antonio) novels, or my La Fontaine fables, or my *Letters from My Windmill,* or my *Diary of a Country Parson*, she said that some of my former pupils still had fond memories of me, that others held positions of national responsibility, had become *somebodies* in various parts of the administration, and that I had actually been the only teacher in that school who didn't belt the pupils, that I was an exemplary man, then she recalled how I'd suddenly been sacked from my teaching post, it's true that was a bleak moment in my existence, but life's like that, was it really my fault, had I really become incapable of teaching my classes, d'you suppose, that was their opinion, the hypocrites, I think I'd better talk about that for a bit now, I ought to say a few words about it, even if my bicycle chicken's been sitting here untouched, growing cold while I'm busy thinking

when I was still teaching I apparently even used to turn up late for classes whenever I'd been drinking, and apparently I even used to show my buttocks to the children in anatomy class, and apparently I even used to draw giant sex organs on the board, and apparently I even used to piss in a corner of the classroom, and apparently I even used to pinch my colleagues' bottoms, male and female, and apparently I even used to offer palm wine round to the pupils, and since there's no such thing as a little problem in this broken world, the regional inspector was informed of my primal behavior, and the regional prefect was also informed of my drifting year, and the prefect at the time was not a man to allow a matter to fester, he would always lance the boil as soon as it appeared, and so this prefect of doom was completely categorical, completely intractable, completely intransigent, and asked quite simply for me to be transferred, he said, in a voice like that of a prophet reading out God's commandments from tablets of stone, "send this drunkard out into the bush, I do not want him anywhere in my district, he's a blight on my campaign against alcohol, I don't want to lose the forthcoming nominations," he was determined to get me switched to the bush, and I said no, in no uncertain terms, no way was I spending my days in the bush peering up the rear end of a chicken, and at that point the district commissioner was informed of the matter, now you don't mess around with a guy over two meters tall, you just do what he says, no discussion, and he agreed with the prefect that I should be parked right out in the bush in among the chickens, and I said no, no, and no again, and at that point the government commissioner was informed, and he was quite a nice guy, he might have been gay, from the way he wiggled his behind like a woman when he walked, and the government commissioner, even though he was quite nice, said the bush was the only answer for people of my stripe, that way I'd only drink palm wine, which, according to him, was less harmful than Sovinco red, and I said, no, no, and no again, and at that point the minister for education was finally informed, and he said "what's this shambles going on down in Trois-Cents, drunkenness is no excuse for idiocy, and vice versa, switch this old soak to the bush and let's hear no more about it," and what happened was it snowballed, the little problem grew into a public row, the bush, or not the bush, that was the question, and all at once the parents began pulling their children out of my classes, and then they wouldn't give me chalk because apparently I even ate that, or crushed it underfoot, and then they wouldn't give me pens because apparently I mistook them for thermometers during lessons and stuck them you know where, and then they wouldn't give me pens or different colored felt-tips because I couldn't tell one color from another, I could only distinguish the red and the black, and they wouldn't give me geometry equipment because apparently I could no longer draw a straight line, which is the shortest distance between A and B, and then they wouldn't give me a map of our country because I still called it by the name it had under royal rule, and I said loud and clear "I don't care, I don't need all that to teach anyway, I'll do it with whatever I've got in hand, you can stuff your pens and stuff your chalk and stuff your map of the country too, because this country's shit, we inherited these borders when the whites carved up their colonial cake in Berlin, so this country doesn't even exist, it's just a reserve, where the cattle die of famine"

and the day came when I turned up in class more than a little drunk, and saw that there was only one pupil sitting at the back of the room, fortunately it was one of my best pupils, and I told him to come forward and sit at the front, he should be proud of his thirst for knowledge, which adorned his angelic brow like a halo, so I began to teach my lesson to this little angel, who looked pityingly at me, because he truly was an angel, with his innocent eyes and understanding gaze, and he stuck with the class, even when his mates failed to show, he sat in the front row, put his things out on the table, his exercise book, his little pocket dictionary, his pencil sharpener, his pencil, his rubber, his pen, and his bottle of water, and I talked to him about plural nouns, it's true I was hammered, but for what it's worth I remember saying "my dear boy, thank you so much for coming, this may be the last time I teach in this school, God has sent you to me, I have a feeling you will be an important man, truly important, and that is why I am going to provide you with the basics of written language, I am going to tell you about plural nouns, which are important in life, my boy, the rest comes after, because life is a banal business of singulars and plurals, locked in daily combat, loving, hating, condemned to live together, so open your exercise book and write down what I tell you, remember this, in general the plural of common nouns is formed by adding an *s* to the end of the word, but watch out because the plural and the singular are the same whenever a word ends in *s, x,* or *z,* such as *bois, noix,* or *nez,* and later we will look at the plurals of compound nouns such as *coffre-fort, basse-cour,* or *tire-bouchon,* and we will also look at the plural of common foreign nouns such as *pizza* or *match*" and just at that point I heard a great uproar outside, a large crowd of people had burst their way in, I turned round, and saw ten or more militiamen, who had entered the classroom and were shouting at me, accompanied by the parents of my last remaining pupil, who was crying, because he didn't want to leave my class, because he wanted to learn the lesson right to the very end, and pursue his education, and not be left in later years, ruing the lost days of childhood, and the militiamen kicked me in the pants and I fought like the very devil, and my pupil was crying and tried to put up a fight to protect me, and I surrendered without a struggle, saying to my little angel, "thank you, little angel, you are better than any of these people casting stones at me, and the reason you are better is because you are the only one who understands me, my cross is heavy, but I shall carry it, uncomplaining, to the bitter end, don't cry now, we will meet again in paradise" and my little angel made a gesture of affection toward me before wiping away his tears, and that was how I got put in quarantine, with an order not to set foot on the school premises, and I said loud and clear "I don't care, doesn't bother me either way" so they suspended me, and I sat around at home for two weeks, then a month, then two months, with no news, and an old lady took over my class, and three or four months later I received a long letter from the administration, which was so badly written I wasted a whole day correcting the grammatical and syntactical errors in it, but in fact what the long letter said was they were offering me another post way up-country, in some far-flung hole where there wasn't even any electricity, even though, as the negroes of our President and General of the Armies would point out, Lenin had quite clearly said *"Communism means Soviet power plus the electrification of the whole country"*

it was during this troubled period that Diabolica begged me to accept the last-ditch solution, saying that the bush wasn't the end of the world, life was cheaper there, you could catch fresh game out the back of your hut, the fish swam gladly into your nets, there the branches of fruit trees were bowed so low that even the garden gnomes complained they had to crouch down as they walked, the bush was good, she argued, there the dead never had to wait in line because there was always room for everyone in the village cemetery, there everyone was friendly, and I said with a naïve air, "oh really, so the bush is great then" and Diabolica sensed that I was revising my position somewhat, and she replied, "Broken Glass, I've been trying to tell you that for days now, you just won't listen, you cling to the town like a baby kangaroo who won't leave his mother's pouch," and I asked in the same breath "then why aren't people rushing to go there, if it's so much better than town?" and she said "because they're idiots, that's why, but you're intelligent, you can understand that the bush means life," and I asked, this time with a worried look, "are you quite sure sending me to the bush wouldn't have something to do with a punishment, then?" and she said she wasn't going to spend the whole day arguing about it, this was the best solution, the right one for both of us, she'll love me, I'll love her, we'll live happily together, away from those who spoke ill of me, were jealous of me, and to conclude the discussion, Diabolica added that if I accepted the proposal she would let me drink as much as I wanted, and promised she would even find someone to bring me palm wine, good quality palm wine every morning, so I immediately felt a great sense of relief, Diabolica only wanted what was best for us, I pictured this idyllic life of ours, me with my bottle of palm wine, and that's why, two days after our fruitful little discussion, part of me thought the bush would be a good idea, while the other part had no wish to leave the town and whispered to me that I was walking into a snare without end, I was really in two minds, to bush or not to bush, that was the question, and during all this time I was thirstier than ever, thirsty for some good Sovinco red, and one day I cracked and went and had a drink, and came home dead drunk as usual, softly singing my favorite song, *Die for your Beliefs,* at the top of my voice, and I could hear that pipe-smoking singer with the mustache singing as if he was singing just for me, and saying in his deep voice "*They were able to convince me, and my cheeky muse, admitted she was wrong, and rallied to their cause, just maintaining a tiny suspicion of doubt,*" and yet I also heard the same singer's warning words, saying "*Now if there's one thing that's really bitter and upsetting, when you offer up your soul to God, it's realizing that you took the wrong turning, got hold of the wrong idea*" and knowing this song by heart I had no wish to take a wrong turning, or get hold of wrong ideas, ideas which would go out of fashion someday, and what the song taught me was that the people who asked others to die for ideas were the last ones to do so themselves, why didn't these moralizers go off and live in the bush themselves then, so I refused to go off into exile up-country, because I didn't want to be a drunk in the bush, and once I had categorically turned down my second chance, the administration seized the opportunity to bar me from public office, they wrote things like "*cher* monsieur, despite our efforts to reach a consensus regarding your current situation it is clear to us that you remain regrettably and resolutely inflexible, adhering obstinately to your position in a manner which leads us to a decision outlined in the provisions governing our national education, a decision with grave consequences indeed, since it obliges us to terminate your employment, this without possibility of appeal, notwithstanding that we propose you be allowed to consider your position for one week, after which, should you have taken no further action, our decision will become active at midnight of the 27th of May, after which date you will have no right to claim either according to article 7b, paragraph e, or to article 34, paragraph f, as amended in the law of the 18th of March 1977" and I said to myself "I don't care, I just couldn't care less, besides, I don't understand a word of this prose anyway" and I went off to tell my new friend the Stubborn Snail about the whole thing, this was around the time when he had problems with the local populace, because of his new venture, and he gave me quite a talking-to, and then said that such was life, one day things are all okay, the next they're not, the important thing was to keep standing tall with your nose to the wind, the important thing was to make the best of this avatar of an absurdly warped version of paradise, I've forgotten which black African poet put it like that, no doubt some guy whose lines many talentless poets have since managed to copy, poor washed-up epigones

I must say Diabolica did not understand my penchant for alcohol, she tried to account for it, she put it down to my mother's death, but what did she know about her death, really, she knew no more than the wagging tongues of Trois-Cents, I preferred her not to mention my mother's death, it really made me mad, I could even turn aggressive, and I've always been in control of my impulses, I've never let anger get the better of me, did she ever hear me criticize her mother, with her one eye bigger than the other, did she ever hear me criticize her father, with his clubfoot and his hernia dangling down between his legs, tell me that, but Diabolica didn't let that bother her, she went on and on about it, waking up my mother's corpse, disturbing her in her search for eternal rest, death's not to be played with like that, we need to put things back in context here, and I actually started drinking well before my mother kicked the bucket, even if I have to admit that her disappearance speeded things up somewhat, but it saddened me to hear Diabolica linking my passion for alcohol to the death of my poor mother, and I felt I really mustn't allow her to draw that particular conclusion, in fact I think I actually consumed rather fewer bottles during the weeks following my mother's disappearance, it was my way of mourning, a mark of respect I owed her, and I only resumed normal activity once I was sure that my mother's corpse had rotted away, and her soul had arrived at last in the garden of Eden

let's say my mother died by drowning in the dirty water of the river Tchinouka, it wasn't her fault, it was all very mysterious, and I'm going to just say a few quick things about it so that things are a bit clearer than the water of the river Tchinouka, because it's important never to confuse one dead person with another, even if the dead all have the same color skin, I mean, just a little word, even if it means my bicycle chicken goes completely cold,

I'll still eat it later, so on the night of her departure for the next world, my mother had a terrible dream, she got up from her bed, eyes closed, mouth wide open, arms stretched out before her as though driven by an invisible force, the shades of the night, and she opened the door of her shack, and went down to the river, hoping to find my father, whom I never knew, it seems he was a highly regarded palm wine tapper in Louboulou, it seems in fact that he had two passions, jazz and palm wine, so those guys like Coltrane, Armstrong, Davis, Monk, Parker, Bechet, and the other negroes who played trumpet and clarinet, he knew all their tunes, which they say were invented in the cotton or coffee fields, to deal with the deep melancholy of their ancestral homeland, and in response, as well, to the whiplashes of their slave-driver masters, who could never understand why the caged bird sang, so anyway, my father was mad for these black men's tunes, it was even said that he collected 33s and 45s of these guys on their trumpets and clarinets, and they say he died from witchcraft at point-blank range, they say someone shot him with a bullet he'd need to have had eyes in the back of his head to avoid, they say he was shot in the back while he slept, because he always slept on his front, even though several sorcerers in Louboulou had warned him not to, and they say it was his uncle who did it, so as to inherit his palm wine tapping tools, not to mention his 33s and 45s of the black men playing their trumpets and clarinets, but the whole story as my mother tried to tell it was too complicated, she wanted to justify her decision to leave the village of Louboulou for the town, she had decided to leave the village where these fine folk lived chiefly to protect me from the witchcraft at point-blank range and from the people who still had it in for my father even though he was dead, and she could see I had my doubts about the story of the nocturnal, mystical gunshot, well, I was less than two years old at the time, and I don't know if I look like my father, people say I look more like the cowardly wretch who killed my progenitor in cold blood and who inherited my father's collection of 33s and 45s of the black men playing their trumpets and clarinets, so my mother's death seemed to me every bit as mysterious as my father's, and at the time she died, the papers called the good woman's death, which was just a small news item, a nocturnal accident, and they ran a headline about the body of an old woman being found on the banks of the river Tchinouka, and that's why whenever I walk by the river I shout abuse at the water, I spit on the ground, I throw stones far, far out, right down into the depths of these vile waters, and rail at the injustice of it all

I set out to talk about my mother, but then the fugitive shade of my father appeared, so to get back to the point, I was saying how my mother's death was also a mystery, she rose from her bed at midnight, in the clutches of a dreadful dream, walked down to the river Tchinouka, and there reenacted in every last detail a scene from the Bible, she walked on the dirty water of the river Tchinouka, as though she might cross over to my father in the other world, and then the dirty water of the river Tchinouka gulped her down into its belly, then spat her back out again like a piece of flotsam on the bank, saying it didn't want her skeletal body in its watery belly, and the local cleaning workers came across her disfigured corpse, nibbled here and there by the small fry in the river and by other fish with no sense of decency, who were hanging around getting bored on the tide of the slimy wave, and the funeral wake was held at our place, on our lot, my mother's body was laid out in the open air, according to the custom of Louboulou, and for this I must thank Diabolica, she looked after my mother very properly, and it was she who sent the contributions card around the neighborhood so that people could support us in our time of grief, and it was she who went to the morgue to identify the body because I don't like looking at corpses, and it was she who led the chorus of women beneath the shelter made of palm leaves, and while they vied in their weeping and their wailing for the dead, Diabolica chased away the nasty flies with their worm-eaten feet, hoping for a look in at my mother's remains, and it was she who supervised the washing of the body, because not just anybody knows how to wash a stiff, and it was she, as well, who sent an obituary notice to the radio station, to announce my mother's death, and it was she who sent out a second communication, thanking everyone who had assisted us during this difficult time, and throughout these days of sadness, Diabolica dressed in black and daubed her face with white clay, and insisted on fasting throughout the funeral time, walking barefoot, leaving her hair uncombed, not looking at men, not talking to me, not saying hello, because that was the custom, and I can only conclude, in all honesty, that from this point of view, she was a woman I have nothing to reproach for, to this day

but it turns out Diabolica always thought that being an only son, who had already lost his father, I took refuge in drink, hoping somehow to get even by drinking red wine, since I'd never be able to save my mother's memory by drinking all the dirty water of the river Tchinouka, and I swear, I wanted to build my life again, fit back together the broken pieces, and mend the holes, and stop spending all my time with the bottle of Sovinco red, but it wasn't my fault, was it, that I'd been fired from my teaching post, I swear I loved teaching, I swear I loved having all my little pupils around me, I swear I loved teaching them their times tables, I swear, too, that I loved teaching them their past participles conjugated with *avoir*, and whether you have to make them agree or not, depending on the time of day and the weather, and the poor little things, dazed, confused, sometimes even angry, would ask me why the past participle does agree today at four o'clock, but didn't yesterday at midday, just before lunch break, and I would tell them that what mattered in the French language was not the rules, but the exceptions to the rules, I would tell them that if they could understand, and memorize all the exceptions in this language, which was as changeable as the weather, then the rules would automatically become apparent, they would be obvious from first principles, and when they were grown up they could forget all about the rules and the sentence structure, because by then they would see that the French language isn't a long, quiet river, but rather a river to be diverted

by rights I should never have been a teacher, I haven't got a secondary-teaching certificate, I never went to teacher-training college, but diplomas can often distort the business of living, a true vocation arises from a combination of circumstances, it's not usually the ones who wear out the seat of their pants at school who become good teachers, and in my case, I was forced into the profession, when I'd only just completed my second year of study at Kengué-Pauline, and the government decreed that since there was a national shortage of teachers, all the poor sods who'd got their elementary-education certificate should go off and teach, and that's how I fell flat-footed into teaching, that's how I came to learn on the job, but in actual fact I taught myself, even though some egghead wearing spectacles came from the political capital to give us intensive training in pedagogy, he fancied himself as an intellectual, said I had no talent, that I didn't speak or pronounce French properly, and the government had made a real blunder, letting ignoramuses like me set our children on the path of life, ever since then I've always hated intellectuals of all kinds, because it's always like that with intellectuals, they talk and talk, but nothing concrete ever comes out of it, only more and more discussions about discussions, then they quote some other intellectuals who said this, that, or the next thing, and who saw it all coming, and then they have a good scratch of their own navels, and they think everyone else is stupid, and blind, as though no one could get through life without philosophizing, and the problem is, these pseudo-intellectuals, they philosophize without actually living, they know nothing about life, and life goes on anyway, following its own course, countering all their second-rate Nostradamus predictions, and they all go round congratulating each other, but what you notice is, pseudo-intellectuals all love suits, and little round glasses, and ties, because an intellectual without a tie is basically stark naked, incapable of proper thought, but I'm proud of how I got here, I did things myself, I'm a self-made man, I don't even know how to tie a tie, but I've read whatever I've been able to get my hands on, and it's obvious no one person could ever read everything, life's not long enough for that, and I've also noticed that there are far more people who talk about bad books than there are people who actually read and talk about real ones, and the people who talk about bad books are merciless about the other ones, well they can just go and get lost, there's more to this world than their little navels, that's not my problem, this book isn't about teaching anyone anything, each of us must cultivate his garden as best he can

I could see why they wanted to fire me from my teaching job, the pretext was alcohol, so, just two months after they did fire me, Diabolica started sleeping at her parents' place, which meant our house was left empty, as we had never had children, and the local thieves and bandits dropped by and looted everything, my TV, my radio, my dining table, my bed, and my books, including my San-Antonio novels, which meant much more to me than the books those people detached from real life told us were the unit of intellectual measurement, and the thieves looted everything, they even took the last book I'd been reading, *Diary of a Thief*, I'm sure they thought there would be stuff in it about learning to steal without getting caught by the police, and Diabolica said the whole thing was my fault, she said it was my drunken friends who stole our things, and I said my friends were drunks but they weren't thieves, and she said I was covering for them, I was their accomplice, and then she left for good, leaving me a scrap of paper on which she'd written, possibly at midnight, "I'm off" and when I turned the paper over, I saw she'd added, possibly also at midnight, "finding an ending," neither of these telegrams meant anything to me, and I looked for her everywhere, in all the backstreets of the district Trois-Cents, in the town center, at funeral wakes, and then one day I saw her walking past Credit Gone West, I thought I was dreaming, and I ran after her and pleaded with her, I said "we were happy," and I also said "I can't live without you, if you leave me I'm fucked, come back home" but she wouldn't change her mind, she looked me up and down and said "you're already fucked, you're not going to change, leave me in peace, you old tramp"

*

I turned into one of Credit Gone West's most loyal customers the year I got thrown out of teaching, I consolidated my friendship with the Stubborn Snail, and became so much part of the fittings and furnishings that the boss said to me "you know, Broken Glass, if you'd been a bit more together, I'd have taken you on as a bartender here" and I replied that I was together and if he doubted the clarity of my mind he could test me on my times tables and he said "no, Broken Glass, business isn't about times tables, it's about clarity of mind" and I said I was perfectly clearheaded and he laughed and we had a drink together and then we laughed some more, there was one tree I would always go and piss under, and tell it my wanderer's tale, and the tree would weep to hear me, because, don't let them tell you otherwise, trees also weep, and sometimes I would shout insults at Diabolica under this tree, and at her mother too, with her one eye smaller than the other, and her father, with his clubfoot and his hernia hanging down between his legs, and when it was really tough, only the tree understood me, and moved its branches, to show that it cared and whispered low that I was a loser, but a nice one, and that society just didn't understand me, and the tree and I would have these long conversations, as the negro would say to his admiral when bringing the water for his coffee, and I promised my leafy friend that when God called me back the next time I would choose to be a tree

I was by now a real regular, and spent my entire time at Credit Gone West, I sat through the hours, come rain or shine, I never left my adopted home, I couldn't imagine being anywhere else, so there I'd be, in the middle of the night, dozing on my stool after eating kebabs sold by an old Benin woman at the entrance to the bar, long before the reign of our dear bald soprano, Mama Mfoa, it was a fine life, and I must make sure to write it down legibly, that I'm proud of those moments of yore, never let it be said I was having a hard time, that I was bored, that I was sad about Diabolica leaving, that I was nursing a grievance, or was planning to write a letter to the friend who did not save my life or to claim a compassion protocol for my trouble

I heard it said, not long ago, that Diabolica was living with a good husband, and they had children, I don't care, there's no such thing as a good husband, I was the man she needed, the rest are just wretched freeloaders and liars who'll exploit her till they've used her up, I'm not jealous, even if I haven't had sex since then, I'm aware that my sex life is a bit like the desert of the Tartars, nothing in front, nothing behind, only the shadows of women talk to me, in truth I'm a man who longs for a distant love, don't expect me to speak to you of love and other demons, fortunately at this unhappy period of my life I still had my love of the bottle, the bottles understood me, they stretched out their arms to me, and whenever I found myself sitting in the bar, which I still love dearly, and always will, I would watch, and observe, and register the doings of the people around me, that's why it's important to explain more exactly why I'm writing this book, to be clear about how and why the Stubborn Snail compelled me to record, witness and pass on the history of this place

in fact the Stubborn Snail took me aside one day and said with a confidential air, "Broken Glass, I want to talk to you about something that's been bothering me, in fact I've been thinking about this for a long time, it's important, I think you should write, I mean, I think you should write a book," and I was rather taken aback and I said "a book on what," and he pointed at the terrace of Credit Gone West and murmured "a book about us, a book about this place, there's no other place like it on earth, except The Cathedral in New-Bell, Cameroon," and I laughed, I thought he must have some other reason, that this was some kind of snare without end, and he said "don't laugh, now, I really mean it, you ought to write, you know you can," and the look on his face told me this was no two-Congolese-franc joke, and I answered "but you're the boss, you're the one who knows what goes on here, I wouldn't know where to start," and he poured me a drink before bouncing back with "believe me, I've tried it a few times myself, but it never works out, I just don't have that little bug that writers have, you have, it shows when you talk about literature, your eyes light up and you look all wistful, but I don't think it's frustration, or bitterness either, because I know you're not at all a frustrated man, or a bitter man, you have no cause for regrets, my friend," and I said nothing, so he went on, "you know, I remember once you told me about a famous writer who drank like a fish, what was his name again," and I didn't answer and he continued "well anyway, since we had that talk, I've been wondering whether you didn't start drinking in imitation of the writer whose name I've forgotten, and come to look at you, you do actually look like a writer, and the reason you don't care much about your life is because you know you can invent all sorts of other lives and you're just one character in the great book of life, of shit and tears, you're a writer, I know, that's why you drink, you are not of this world, some days I get the feeling you're deep in conversation with those guys like Proust or Hemingway, guys like Labou Tansi or Mongo Beti, I can tell you are, so you should just let yourself go, you're never too old to write," and for the first time ever I saw him knock back his drink in one gulp, whereas normally he only ever drinks half a glass, and he said with a military air "Broken Glass, I want your inner anger out from inside you, go on, explode, vomit, spit, cough, or ejaculate, I don't care how you do it, just turn out something about this bar for me, about some of the guys who hang out here, and especially about yourself," for a moment his words stopped the words in my mouth, I felt like crying, I couldn't remember which drunken writer it was we'd talked about, in any case, quite a lot of them drank, and some writers today drink lethal amounts, what had got into the Stubborn Snail that day, needling down deep inside me, huh, so in my own defense I said over and over, "I'm not a writer, and besides, who'd want to read about these people's lives, or mine, there's no interest in that, you'd never fill a whole book," and he came straight back saying, "who cares, Broken Glass, you've got to write, it's interesting to me, for a start," and I felt proud that he'd asked me, and actually the idea began to take shape in my head from that point on, fueled by one glass of red after another, I outlined my real thoughts about writing to the Stubborn Snail, and it was simple to express myself, because it is easy to talk about writing when, like me, you've written nothing, and I told him that in this crappy country everyone thinks he can turn his hand to writing, even when there's no life behind the words, and I told him that sometimes on the TV in a bar on the Avenue of Independence I'd see some of those writers who wear jackets and ties, bright red scarves, sometimes round glasses, smoking pipes or cigars, trying to look good, like smart young things, the kind of writers who take photos looking as though they've got great works under their belts and all they want people to talk about is their own navels, the size of a clockwork orange, some of them even fancy themselves neglected writers, convinced of their own genius, when they've produced nothing but sparrows' droppings, they're paranoid, embittered, jealous, envious, always convinced there's some great conspiracy against them, and they say that even if one day they did win the Nobel Prize for literature, they'd categorically turn it down, they don't want to find themselves with dirty hands, the Nobel Prize for literature is a mesh, a wall, iron in the soul, the bets have already been placed, to the point where you start wondering what *is* literature, and yes all these crappy writers would turn down the Nobel Prize in order to preserve the road to freedom, I'll believe that when I see it, and I also said to the Stubborn Snail that if I was a writer I would ask God to grant me the gift of humility, to give me the strength to put my own writing into perspective alongside the giants of this world who have put pen to paper, and that I would say three cheers for true genius, and would keep silent rather than speak of the mediocrity all around us, and that would be the only way you could hope to write something remotely like real life, but I'd say it in my own words, twisted words, incoherent words, nonsensical words, I'd write down words as they came to me, I'd begin awkwardly and I'd finish as awkwardly as I'd begun, and to hell with pure reason, and method, and phonetics, and prose, and in this shit-poor language of mine things would seem clear in my head but come out wrong, and the words to say it wouldn't come easy, so it would be a choice between writing or life, that's right, and what I really want people to say when they read me is "what's this jumble, this mess, this muddle, this mishmash of barbarities, this empire of signs, this chitchat, this descent to the dregs of belles lettres, what's with this barnyard prattle, is this stuff for real, and where does it start, and where the hell does it end?" and my mischievous answer would be "this jumble of words is life, come on, come into my lair, check out the rotting garbage, here's my take on life, your fiction's no more than the output of a load of old has-beens designed to comfort other old has-beens, and until the day your characters start to see how the rest of us earn our nightly crust, there'll be no such thing as literature, only intellectual masturbation, with you all rubbing up against each other like donkeys," and to sum up I said to the Stubborn Snail that, sadly, I wasn't a writer, I could not be a writer, all I ever did was watch the world, and talk to my bottles and to my tree, the one I like to piss under, to whom I had made a promise to come back in vegetal form, and live a new life alongside it, and because of that I would rather leave the job of writing to the intellectually gifted, the writers I so loved to read in the days when I still read in order to learn, I would leave writing, I said, to those who sing of the joy of life, who struggle, and who dream without ceasing of the extension of the domain of the struggle, those who invent fancy ways of dancing the polka, those who can astonish the gods, those who wallow in disgrace, those who walk steadfastly toward manhood, those who create a practical dream, those who sing of the land without shadows, those who live in transit in one corner of the earth, those who see the world through an attic window, those who, like my late father, listen to jazz and drink palm wine, those who can describe an African summer, those who tell tales of barbarous weddings, those who retreat to the summit of the magic rock of Tanios, and pass their time in meditation, I told him I'd leave writing to those who remind us that too much sun kills love, those who prophecy the sobbing of the white man, phantom Africa, the innocence of the black child, I told him I'd leave writing to those who can construct a town inhabited by dogs, who can put up a green house like the Printer's or a house on the edge of tears to shelter the humble and homeless, those who sense the compassion of stones, yes, I told him, I'd leave writing to them, and rule out the nutters and the live wires, the weekend poets with their threepenny verses, and it's just bad luck on the nostalgic Senegalese riflemen, who tear to shreds the very core of militancy, and the guys who think a black man shouldn't speak of birch trees, of stone, of dust, of winter, of snow, of a rose, or simply of beauty for beauty's sake, and rule out the integrationalist imitators that pop up like mushrooms, how many are their number, who congest the highway of letters, sully the purity of the universe, and pollute the true literature of our time

when I said all this to the Stubborn Snail, he was lost for words, he thought I must be angry with someone in particular, or that I was raving, and he said who was I talking about, he wanted names, but I didn't reply, I just smiled and gazed up at the sky, and he kept at me to know if I was angry and I said no, why should I be angry, I had no cause to be angry, I was just setting things straight, just making a distinction between what I considered rubbish, and what I thought was good, and that was the day he gave me this notebook, and a pencil and said "if you change your mind you could always write in this, it's your book, it's a present, I know you will write, just write what you feel like, the kind of thing you were saying just now, about true writers and fake writers that congest the highway of literature, and about the people who turn down the Nobel prize and the nostalgic Senegalese riflemen, and the writers you saw in suits on TV in the bar on the Avenue of Independence, that's all good stuff, you can work on that, find a way to grab me as a reader, yes, I want to read about all that, I'm not quite sure what you meant by it, but I still think you need to put down everything you've just said" so since then, to please him, I've been writing down my stories in the book, my rough impressions, and sometimes I do it for my own pleasure too, and that's when I really feel like I'm hitting my stride, when I let myself go, and forget this is something I've been asked to do, I feel at ease in the saddle, I can buck and jump and I can talk to a reader other than the Stubborn Snail, a reader I've never met, because anything can happen, and the Stubborn Snail did say to me once "I promise not to read what you write until the day you reach the last full stop," my book is always here ready for me, and there are days when I say to Mompéro or Dengaki, "bring me two bottles of red and my notebook" and they bring me my two bottles and my notebook and I drink and I scribble away and watch the world, let's just say that until now I've been happy that way, a happy man, a free man, but it makes me feel pretty sad to think that in future I won't be scribbling away in my book, and I won't be turning up here in days to come, so I need to look back a bit over what I've written so far, and I mustn't forget to finish my bicycle chicken, which has gone quite cold, because I took my time over the story of my life, when I should have been eating, but I think it was necessary, so now I'm going to just stop for a bite to eat, I'm actually starving, though I may not look it

I finally managed to eat my bicycle chicken, and now I have to go and give the plate back to the bald soprano on the other side of the Avenue of Independence, but first I'll drink up my glass of red wine, which will only take a few seconds, besides, time doesn't matter now, I see the Printer's still here, still surrounded by people flicking through the latest *Paris Match*, well I don't care, it's nothing to do with me, I'm busy anyway, and I stand up and get ready to cross the Avenue of Independence, I'll manage all right, there's not two-way traffic, unless I've gone blind, and there are no motorcycles either, and no garbage trucks that I can see, ah, there we are, it's done, I've made it, I can claim a victory now, it wasn't a foregone conclusion, so I'm across the avenue, and I can see the bald soprano, she can see me walking toward her, she smiles, she's always smiling, I'm standing before her, she smiles again and quips, "well now, Broken Glass, you took your time eating today, weren't you hungry then, just look at you now, you're fit to drop, ooh, how many liters you got under your belt there papa" and I say I've not started drinking yet, I've not touched a drop of alcohol since I got up this morning, and I laugh even as I utter this lie, which is as big as an African dictator's second home, but I can see she doesn't believe me, because she says "when d'you ever meet a drunk who'll admit he's been drinking, never, that's when, papa, there's a song about that, it goes "*momeli ya massanga andimaka kuiti te mama*," it's not a song I know, she says it's by a band called Almighty OK Jazz, an amazing band from the country over the way, I don't know much about this country's music, just a few songs by Zaiko Langa Langa, and Afrisa International, that's all, and I come clean and say "well, yes, Mama Mfoa, I did have just one little glass, a really small one, no more, I promise" and the look she gives me is full of kindness, I've never seen her look so serious in all the time I've known her and she shakes her head and murmurs "I told you to give up drinking, Broken Glass, you're going to die with a bottle in your hand, papa, we all care about you here in the district" and I can't think what to say to her right now, so I say, without thinking "I'll stop tonight, at midnight, I give you my word, I promise, Mama Mfoa, and I'll never show my face round here again" and I'd really like to tell her that I'm not stopping drinking because I'm afraid of dying, I'm not scared that I'll die with a bottle in my hand, the truth is, it's a good way to go, it's what they call dying with your weapon in your hand, because when we pass through to heaven or hell we know anything can happen, when we get there everything depends on which strait gate we each go through, I expect some people will go in through the wrong gate, in heaven it's all very serious, lots of white clouds and angels with the memories of elephants, asking you how many times you've read the Jerusalem Bible, how many old ladies you've helped across the Avenue of Independence, which churches you attended down below, no way you'll get a drink up there, it's one big oral exam, strictly no drinking in paradise, and in hell it's much the same, it'll be just as hard to get a drop to drink there, what with the devil hanging around between a rock and hard place prodding us with his trident, and if you ask him for a drop of wine he'll turn angry and shout "what's that, what d'you want from me, idiot pain in the ass, don't you think you drank enough down below without coming pestering us here in purgatory, you should have aimed for paradise, aimed a little higher, beyond those dark clouds over there, well, bad luck, you should have drunk your fill on earth, while you still had the chance, all you'll get here is your judgment, with no appeal, here the crackling flames of the apocalypse rule the day, incineration with no deliberation, no alcohol to be consumed on the premises, we just use it to light the flames and make them leap, come now, your turn to burn, poor fool, who believed hell was other people"

I'd just like to point out I'm not a bad man, nor hysterical, or anything like that, no, no one's going to call me that, even if I do plan to throw in the towel at the stroke of midnight, I'm a sensible man, otherwise how come those people who say they're not drunks can't do their times tables, huh, I mean, anyone can multiply by two, but once you start multiplying by nine, say, it does get tricky, and then there's decimals and all that jazz, but I've never given in to the temptation to count on my fingers, or with sticks, and I've certainly never even set eyes on a calculator, I don't give a damn about modern math, to me life means a bottle and the multiplication tables, just as for my father, life meant jazz and palm wine, Coltrane, Monk, Davis, Bechet and all the other negroes, with their trumpets and clarinets, God himself told us to go forth and multiply, though he didn't actually specify how much we should multiply by, but he did bid us go forth and multiply, I really like multiplication, even if I've always been keener on geography and literature, it's true I couldn't have taken literature any further, even if I'd carried on with my studies, literature leads nowhere, geography would have just about been okay, I could have traveled the world with it, I could have studied the great rivers in all their length and breadth, the river Congo, the river Amour, the Yangtze-Kiang, or the Amazon, but I've never seen these rivers with my own eyes, the only river I've ever known is dark red in color and comes in a bottle, and this river, of the color purple, will never run dry, no more than the ones I've just named, and when I think about the liters of wine I've drunk over the past twenty years, if that's not a long quiet river, I don't know what the world's coming to, anyway, I'm not going to get bogged down in hydrographic detail here, water is a dangerous element, and it still makes me furious to think of my mother swallowing great mouthfuls of water before she finally surrendered her spirit, with no time even to say *"our Father, who art in heaven"*

I'll just make a note here, without wishing to boast, that one way or another I've traveled the world, I wouldn't want anyone to think I'm one of those guys who doesn't know what's going on outside his native country, that would be too narrow a view, just because I'm filled to the gills with red wine doesn't mean I've forgotten the exploits of my youth, it would be fairer to say I have traveled widely, without ever leaving my own native soil, I've traveled, one might say, through literature, each time I've opened a book the pages echoed with a noise like the dip of a paddle in midstream, and throughout my odyssey I never crossed a single border, and so never had to produce a passport, I'd just pick a destination at random, setting my prejudices firmly to one side, and be welcomed with open arms in places swarming with weird and wonderful characters, was it perhaps by chance that all my wandering started with comic strips, perhaps not, because one day, I found myself in a Gallic village, alongside Asterix and Obelix, then another time out in the Far

West, with Lucky Luke, the cowboy who shoots faster than his own shadow, I marveled at the adventures of Tintin, at his skill in giving people the slip, at his little dog, Snowy, an intelligent hound, ever ready to help his master should the need arise, now you don't find dogs like him in Trois-Cents, the dogs around here are only interested in grubbing up knucklebones to chew from the public garbage heap, they have no power of reasoning, and then there was Zembla, who thrust me back deep into the jungle, as did Tarzan, that bundle of muscle, swinging from creeper to creeper, and then there was our friend Zorro, wielding his skillful sword, while the envious Isnogud longed to be caliph instead of the caliph, I shall never forget my first trip across an African country, it was Guinea, I was the black child, I was entranced by the blacksmiths' toil, so intrigued by the creep of the mystical snake who swallowed a reed that I felt like I held it in my hands, then suddenly I'd be back in my native country, eating sweet, sweet fruit of the breadfruit tree, living in a room of a hotel called *Life and a Half*, which no longer exists, but where my father spent his evenings in a state of bliss, with his jazz and his palm wine, and I warmed myself by the fire of my origins, but almost at once I must be off again, I mustn't get trapped by the warmth of my native soil, I must wend my way through the rest of the continent listening to the major elegies and shadow songs, and trail through brutal cities in the hope of meeting one last survivor of the caravan, yes I really must go, and travel northward, and experience the highest solitude, see the diverted river, and live in the big house filled with the light of an African summer, and leave this continent, to discover other hot countries, and live one hundred years of solitude, adventures and discovery in a village called Macondo, fall under the spell of a character called Melquiades, and listen entranced to tales of love, madness, and death, pass discreetly through the tunnel which leads to the understanding of human emotion, but first I had to open the greenhouse, and then even go to India to listen to Tagore, the sage, chanting his *Gora,* I must cast my net across the entire continent of Europe, so dear to our friend the Printer, I, the outsider, the rebel, the approximate man, I was just behind a guy called Doctor Zhivago who walked through the snow, it was the first time I'd seen what snow looked like, and there was this other guy in exile in Guernsey, I felt sorry for him, an old ancient with his face all riddled with lines, he never stopped writing, and doing drawings in India ink, he was inexhaustible, with bags of flesh beneath his eyes, he didn't even hear me coming, and over his shoulder I read about the punishments he'd planned to inflict on the monarch who was looking for him, on whose account he couldn't sleep, and whom he'd nicknamed *Napoleon le Petit,* I envied him his grey hair, he was truly somebody, I envied his flowing patriarchal beard, this man whose life spanned the century, apparently even as a child he said *"I want to be Chateaubriand or nothing"* and I admired his unswerving gaze, which I'd noticed before in an old Lagarde and Michard, which was my basic textbook back when I was a man like all the rest, and I found myself standing in his home, the Feuillantines, I had crossed the garden and hidden among the roses, and from there I was able to spy on the rebellious and womanizing grandfather, his back was stooped, his nose buried in a sheaf of scattered papers, which he was nervously correcting, sometimes he left off writing poems and began drawing hangmen, I was only a few steps from his house, I watched as he got to his feet, with difficulty, his work had exhausted him, he wanted to leave the house, walk for a while, just to stretch his legs, so I hid, not wishing to meet his gaze, and I left that place, and came back to Trois-Cents, from where I would often make a trip to the Atlantic Ocean, to cadge a few sardines from the Beninese fishermen, till the day I thought I saw an albatross, an ungainly bird, with wings which ached from his constant circling above the roaring waves, and who with his flight drew figures in the air, outlining the lands he had visited and the ships he had followed, and suddenly, close to the fishermen's shacks, I saw a thin and wizened old man who said to me in a hoarse voice "young man, allow me to introduce myself, my name is Santiago, I'm a fisherman, my little boat is always empty, but I love to fish," and alongside Santiago was a little boy, who was saddened to see him coming home each evening with an empty boat, but I had to go, I had to move on, that's how I've always been, always searching for something I couldn't name, I haven't the stamina I used to have, my strength of mind has withered with the years, and now I drift like a lump of filth caught in the current of a diverted river last time, I think it was the day I said I was going to have a bit of a rest and not write for a while, and before I left the bar I saw the Saviem truck that delivers our red wine arrive, I saw the racks of red wine stacked way high, and there were some enfants terribles running around it, and I thought to myself what a real shithole this country has become, with enfants terribles swarming round barrels of wine, and then one of the guys chased them away from the precious load, saying red wine wasn't meant for enfants terribles, they'd have to wait till they were of age, and for the time being they'd have to make do with grapefruit juice, and Guigoz baby formula, or Bébé Hollandais or Bledilac and toys appropriate to their tender years, and the enfants terribles left in a terrible huff, and I began daydreaming about which of the thousands of bottles before me would be the first to wend its weary way down my gullet, while the man from the warehouse was unloading it with an air of detachment, which drove me crazy, in fact his attitude toward the bottles by means of which he earned his daily—and nightly—bread was downright disrespectful, I felt sorry for those bottles, there they were, rattling against each other, jostling for position, digging each other hard in the ribs, without getting out of line, and the man from the warehouse piled them all up neatly beside me, and I took a bottle at random and indicated to the Stubborn Snail that I'd pay for it later that day, not tomorrow, and he said "no problem, Broken Glass, if it's you I'm not worried, if it was anyone else I'd say, credit is dead, it's long since gone away," now that's real friendship, the friendship you get between me and the Stubborn Snail

so while I was sitting there minding my own business the day the delivery came to Credit Gone West, the guy who wears four thick layers of Pampers on his butt came and stuck his red nose round the door of the bar, looking a bit like Zapatta the clown, I don't know where he'd popped up from, Pandora's box, I expect, but there he was in front of me, panting slightly, his hair all disheveled, and his skin coated in dust, like a candidate at a voodoo ceremony, he had only one shoe on, and spit was dribbling out of his mouth, as though he'd talked too much that day, he looked quite altered, a different man altogether, and at first I didn't want to look at him, standing there like a child who's just had a clementine snatched out of his hand, no, I really didn't want to look at him, he looked so like a man haunted by a childhood photograph, and then there were all these flies buzzing after his behind, and he rushed up to me as though he'd had a dream about me, as though I was the very person he'd come to see, and he stood stock-still in front of me, like a pillar of salt, and at last I made myself look at him, he looked strange, very strange indeed this time, you'd have thought someone had asked him to solve the problem of squaring the circle and he'd come to ask me for help, maybe that was what made me think I should back off as quickly as possible, so the Pampers guy sat down beside me, without speaking, he sat down like a zombie come back from down among the dead men and I said nothing, "where are you up to with your notebook, I hope you've written my story down," he said, and I nodded, but he didn't look as though he believed me, and he fixed his eyes on my notebook, so I closed it straightaway, and he started to tell me the story about his wife all over again, all about the lock being changed, and the fire brigade, and the police, particularly the police officer of the feminine persuasion who had put the handcuffs on him, and I was only half listening because I'd already finished telling his story and hearing the same old record twice over is a real drag, and he said to me "are you listening, or not, Broken Glass, I'm talking to you, man" and I replied "of course I'm listening, my friend, it's a sad story, you're a trooper, I really admire your courage, it's not everyone has your courage," and he said "why aren't you putting down what I'm saying now, though, you're all fine words, you think that will make me feel better, but in actual fact you don't give a damn about my story, you don't give a damn about the rather droll story of a poor fool's ruin, well let me tell you, I paid for everything in that house, electricity, water, rent, you don't believe me do you, go on, tell me you do, shit, say something, Broken Glass, say anything" and I said "my friend, I am interested in your story, I'd never ever make fun of you, believe me," and he said "so what do you think about it then, what do you say to this crazy tale of mine, what do you think, tell me honestly, take at look at me now, am I an idiot, do I really look like a fool?" and I replied "life lies all before us, you know, even if your wife has behaved badly and even if she's still fornicating with the guru from that damned sect, life lies all before us" he gave a start, as though I'd just hurt him, or insulted him, "what are you on about, Broken Glass" and I thought he was going to leap on me, so I said quietly, "I was simply reminding you that your wife is a witch, forget her, the file's closed, you're not an idiot, you don't look like a fool, you're a sensible guy, you're generous and open, I can't even find the right words to describe you, but you're a good man," but it was just as though I'd thrown oil on the fire, the guy suddenly raised his voice loud and said "hey, Broken Glass, I'm not going to let you insult my ex-wife like that, what do you mean she's a witch, what do you mean she's sleeping with the guru on the TV, what do you mean she's a bad woman, if you think that, then you didn't understand a word I told you last time, I want to read your book now, I thought as much, I'm disappointed in you, Broken Glass, truly disappointed," and I didn't understand what he was saying, he was really starting to bug me, here he was, defending a woman who'd thrown him out, a woman who'd had him put in prison, a woman whose fault it was that his ass was going to ooze for all eternity, and so I said to him in a conciliatory voice, "I thought you were angry with your wife, but it turns out you still love her," and he added "of course I love her, what do you think, why did you say the file was closed, I still love her, and soon I'll be a man like other men again, my backside will dry up, I won't have to wear diapers, and I'll go and win my wife back, we'll have a new romance, no drums, and I'll write her poems about the lily and the paradise flower, I'll take her on a trip to Kinshasa, across the river, after all, we've got six children together, that's not to be sneezed at, I trusted you, I told you about my life, and you just make fun of me, you say the file's closed, I know deep down you're laughing at me, give me that book, I want to read it, if you don't give it to me things are going to get nasty between you and me, and I want you to rub out everything you've written about me, I don't want people to know my story" and then I was stuck for what to say to him, I needed to think of something, to defuse the atmosphere a bit, and I mumbled "listen, man, I'm really happy to hear you talking like that, in any case, I'm right with you, believe me, I would never make fun of you" but he didn't see it the same way, he hit straight back with "oh no, Broken Glass, you don't really mean that, you don't mean it at all, I can tell, don't do that to me, don't fake it, that's going to really annoy me, things are going to get nasty between you and me, believe me, give me that book" and I stood up, I put the book on my stool and I sat down on it, that way he couldn't grab it off me, I was surprised, I was shocked, I couldn't believe it was the same guy talking to me like this, and I said "what's going on, my friend, is there some problem between us?" and then, since he was really starting to bug me, I got out my big guns and came on heavy, saying "you want me to spell it out, you prick, okay, I wish those guys at the prison in Makala had gone even harder at your backside, I wish they'd stuck it right up into your mouth" I just came out with it like that because I was really on edge and he immediately answered "what about you then, d'you think I don't know your story, then, well I do, I know everything and I hope you've got the guts to write that one down in your notebook too, because it's all very easy to talk about other people and not about yourself, but I know who you are, you're a hypocrite, a real hypocrite, you're pathetic, you're a loser, you sit around here playing the sage, but really you're nothing, just nothing," that's what he said, and there he was really taking it just that bit too far, I wanted to calm things down a bit, so I said "my friend, what's got into you today, I only want what's best for you, let's discuss it like grown-ups," and he gave me the finger and came back with "you go fuck yourself, you old scoundrel, you bush toad" so there was nothing else for it, I had no choice, and I said to him, "man, I can have you thrown out of here, d'you know that the Stubborn Snail's a personal friend of mine," "yeah, he's a personal friend of mine too, and a personal friend of everybody's" was his reply, then he added with a scornful look, "I know about you, Broken Glass, I know your story from start to finish, you can't fool me, weren't you the one who showed your backside to the children during lessons, and while we're at it, what about your mother, eh, yeah, let's talk about her, she was just one of the local drunks, an old wreck who drowned in the River Tchinouka, let's face it, you're the pedophile around here, not me, that's why you were thrown out of Trois-Martyrs School, because you soiled the cloakroom of childhood, you nipped the buds, shot the kids" this guy was really trying to rile me, he wanted me to lose it, how could he possibly call me a pedophile, how did he dare sully my mother's memory, had he ever actually seen her then, my mother's my mother, as far as I'm concerned she's not dead, she's still here inside me, she speaks to me, she guides me, she protects me, I couldn't let him get away with an outrageous slur like that, who did he think he was, and I felt my heart, my heart began to swell and I was trembling, I felt a snake in my fist, I mumbled bitter words "O rage, O despair, Have I then lived so long only for this disgrace" but it was no good, I was quite beside myself with anger, and I said "get the hell out of this bar then, you walking bag of bones, you wreck of the peninsula" and he answered "I'm not budging, you're not the boss, you old fool, you better back out now, your time's up, make way for the next generation!" and at that I was on my feet in three seconds flat, like some couple dancing a tango of hate, I spun round on my heels, I grabbed him by his tattered shirt collar, suddenly I felt strong again, the force was with me, I felt myself about to roar and bark and growl like thunder, I shook him like a crappy bottle of Orangina and sent my viper fist flying into his face, he didn't see the viper fist coming, and people started shouting, some of them said I should go ahead and really beat him up, with his ass that would be damp for the rest of his days, and the guy shat in his pants because when I've got my snake in my fist like that, I'm really dangerous, it's a gris-gris my mother made for me when I was very small, because I was an only son, she didn't want people beating me up at school, and anyone who's ever had my viper fist in their face know how much it hurts, it's like a scythe, and I knocked that Pampers guy flat, we went down on the floor, and rolled in the dust right as far as the edge of the Avenue of Independence, not far from the bald soprano, and I think the whole district must have come out into the street, and the spectators were shouting "Ali, *bomayé,* Ali, *bomayé,* Ali, *bomayé*" because I was Muhammed Ali and he was George Foreman, and I was floating like a butterfly, I was stinging like a bee, and he was a flat-footed vegetable, and I could see his punches coming and was dodging them neatly, and when we came to blows I had the upper hand straightaway, because the other guy was just a black-market vegetable, I was kicking him, head butting him, sometimes it hurt me, but he took it, and my punches came raining down on him, there was no stopping me, and he thought he must be surrounded, that there must be five or six guys fighting him, and his nose was bleeding, he was calling to his mother for help, he wanted to run for it, but I held him back, I was pushing him, I was turning him around, I had him biting the dust, and the Stubborn Snail came out of the bar with a cloth over his left shoulder and came running toward us, pushing people aside, "let me through, it's nothing, get outta here you guys" and the crowd booed him, because they appeared to be enjoying the spectacle of our misfortune, the Stubborn Snail separated us and got us to sit down at a table and said "now what's this crazy business you two, I don't want this kind of thing in my bar, why are you fighting like madmen, you want to make more trouble for me, you want me to lose my license or what, for fuck's sake, you're both adults, you're acting like kids, we've never had trouble at Credit Gone West, the authorities are going to start saying it's a free-for-all around here, they're going to close down the bar, I don't want none of this nonsense round here, d'you understand" and I said "I swear to you, he was the one that started it, I never wanted a fight" and he said "that's not true, I swear, it was him that started it, old Broken Glass over there, I didn't want a boxing match, I just wanted to stop him writing about my life" and I said "you should be ashamed telling lies like that" and he said "you're the liar round here, you write all kinds of stuff about people, what d'you think you are then, some kind of writer or something" and we almost started fighting again, but the boss shouted, "stop, both of you, that's enough of that, I don't even want to know about it, you just take these two bottles and make friends again, shake hands, and be quick about it" and we did shake on it, and everyone clapped, even the people standing outside waiting for battle to recommence, and we had a drink with the Pampers guy, and we forgot about the whole incident, and I picked up my notebook off the floor and went for a walk round the block

each of us has his own worries, but the Pampers guy sure has had some really big ones hanging round his neck since the dawn of time, I never set out to provoke anyone, I've often said that, and it was the first row I'd ever had here, and that's why I thought it was time to throw in the towel, I could have gone on many more rounds, I wasn't played out, I shouldn't let idiots like him screw up my life, my empire of the clouds, I'll stand proudly on stage, as it is in heaven, guardian of the ruins of this place, we all have our shit to shovel, the guy must have a truly litigious intelligence quotient, he thought I couldn't kick him up the ass, just because I'm a precious antique, and what he discovered was, a dinosaur's a dinosaur for all that, so ever since the fight I've resolved not to listen to him and his shitty story, I very nearly tore out all the pages about his death on credit and set fire to them, but I decided it would be interesting to leave them and to write up our little falling-out, because it's important to spice things up a bit so the reader doesn't doze off, but I don't speak to the Pampers guy now, I've adopted a new philosophy in life which is simple and to the point, tell every painter he's a genius, or he'll fly at your throat, but I've forgotten who it was coined these fine words of wisdom, some well set-up guy, I expect, some serious guy who honored the memory of his late mother, and thought she was a real belle du seigneur, so the Pampers diapers, the changed lock, the police officer of feminine persuasion, to hell with all that claptrap it's nothing to do with me now, I won't be hearing any more about it

I've just asked a weird-looking guy sitting drinking a couple of tables away for the time, I haven't seen him here before, he's got a book in his hand, the title's in English, not a language I speak, but I can see a drawing on the front cover of a raging horse, from here I can't read the whole title, I can only read the words *in the Rye*, the rest is hidden by the man's enormous hands, but I ask him the time anyway, and he takes a good look at me, smiles as though he knows me, and tells me somewhere between six and six-thirty, and since I really don't like that kind of neither-here-nor-there reply, I say "that's a funny way to tell someone what time it is, either it's six in the evening or six-thirty" and he looks me up and down, and says quite clearly "why don't you just go and fuck yourself, you old lush, your hair's turned white while you've been sitting here, you stink of shit, what you doing hanging round here, you should be reading the tales of Amadou Koumba or Mondo to your grandsons instead of sitting around here looking at other people, writing whatever it is you're writing in your shitty notebook there," I couldn't answer him straight off, he was so obviously trying to pick a Querelle of Brest with me, and I said to myself times change, customs differ, here come the *margouillats* wagging their heads at the aged lion who asks only for a little respect and consideration, and here sits the aged lion, getting kicked by Aliboron, the mangy ass" and I had an urge to shut him up, the pompous jerk, and again I felt the viper in my fist, like the day I got into a row with the Pampers guy, but there's no point, surely there are more important things in life, why waste your time with people who read books in English, after all, but I was so angry I had to say something, and I said "young man, who d'you think you are to talk to me like that?" and he sits looking at me for a while before he says "I'm new here, my name's Holden" and I shake my head, I think to myself that a while ago I would have been interested in this guy, he'd open up to me, he'd read me the user's manual to his shitty life, his disappointment with his little world, because he's out of another age, this guy, he must think he's still living in the postwar era, but I lost all interest in these heartrending stories, and this guy who calls himself Holden, he's weird, he looks like an adolescent in crisis, though he must be getting on for at least thirty, something like that, he's really plump, his face is all puffy, he's got holes in his shoes, he's no stranger to the way the knife of destiny has wounded the lives of the clients of this bar, anyway, I don't care now, I don't have to listen to anyone anymore, and I look away from him, but the guy keeps at me, and says "I'm going to ask you a question, since you're so wise, and so old," so he really knows how to get me interested, and I wonder what kind of question he might ask me, I anticipate the worst, and he puts his question, saying "can you tell me what happens to the poor little ducks in cold countries during winter, do they get put in the zoo, or do they migrate to other countries or do the poor little ducks get stuck in the snow, I want to know what you think" and I look at him and my eyes are wide in disbelief, he must be taking the piss, he's really the craziest of the lot, and I have to walk past him now, so I just say in passing "I don't want to listen to you, I don't want to listen to anyone in this bar anymore, I've had enough, I don't give a shit about the ducks, I don't give a shit if they put them in cages, or if they die in the snow, or migrate to other countries" and I turn my back on him, and he comes back at me again "you better listen to me Broken Glass, that's an order, I want my place in your book, it's not fair if you don't mention me, some really interesting things have happened in this rotten life of mine, and believe me, I'm the most important guy who comes in here, I've done America" and I say to him, "you might as well save your breath, you won't win my heart with those tricks, I've already had someone else come up and tell me he was the most important because he'd done France," and he says "yeah, but I've come from far away, really far away, that's different," "I don't give a damn, my friend, you can't come from farther away than me, Broken Glass," and he shouted, "what d'you mean, are you trying to say you come from far away, when you've never even been in a plane, that's a laugh, if there's anyone who's stood as still as a mountain round here, it's you," and I don't answer, I walk off a little, "come on then, d'you want me to tell you my story or not?" "no thank you, my cup is full," and I move off another two meters, and he shouts "I come from far away, really far away, I spent part of my childhood in America," and I say to him, "America is never going to make me change my mind," and I turn my back on him once and for all while he's still muttering "shit, America's America, the greatest power in the world, I don't care what it takes, you'll listen to me in the end, you'll write down my American story, your book will be good for nothing if you don't, absolutely nothing, only toilet paper," I hear him shouting after me, "hey, Broken Glass, I'm not kidding, I really want your answer, can you tell me what happens to the poor little ducks in the cold countries when winter comes, do they put them in zoos, do they migrate to other countries, or do they just get stuck in the snow"

I look up from my notebook and glance over at the entrance, I don't believe it, here comes Robinette, she's braided her hair, which is normally really wild, she's wearing new wraps, her backside imprisoned in an amazing Dutch wax *pagne*, the Stubborn Snail gives an irritating smile, he looks like he thinks I should get myself in there, tell Robinette how I feel about her, but I'm not doing that, no way, I couldn't do that, it's not worth it now, but she comes walking past me, I look at her for a moment, she clocks me, and says "what you checking me out for like that, you want my photo or what?," and I say "I don't know what you're talking about, Robinette, I hadn't even noticed you were there," she points her finger at me and shouts, "liar, you gunning for me or what, I see, just because I'm dressed up like this, you think men don't notice me, you're gunning for me, oh yes you are, Broken Glass," "I promise, I didn't see you, but that doesn't mean the other men here didn't see you, I'm just me, nobody else," and she shouts again "shit, you make me angry, now you're really making me angry, why didn't you see me then, eh, why didn't you see me, I don't care about other men, I want to know why You didn't see me," "well, actually I did see you really, but I pretended not to see you, so you wouldn't know I'd seen you, that's why," she says "you mean to say I'm fat, is that it, that's why you pretended not to see me, I'm fat, that's it, go on, tell the truth," hey, why are they all starting to gang up on me, could it be they've realized that, as patriarch of this place, I am approaching the autumn of my days, and now everyone's got an opinion about me, they're not afraid of me now, they think I'm finished, not worth a kopeck now, not a single Congolese franc, and I do feel rather as though I've grown old, that the years weigh heavy on my shoulders, that there's nothing more to live for, everything irritates me, that I'm losing the thread, feeling vulnerable now, that when an ass kicks me below the belt I can't kick back, first there was the guy in Pampers, doing my head in with the endless story of his wife changing the lock at five in the morning, and while I'm busy sympathizing like an honest soul, or like Ulysses' faithful dog, he has the nerve to assault my mother's memory, and when we started fighting I felt a viper in my fist and then there was the Printer, even if things hadn't turned sour with the guy in Pampers, but the Printer was really stirring it with his *Paris Match*, it's just one thing after another, today there was the guy with the puffy face who says he comes from America and claims his name is Holden, worrying about what happens to ducks in winter, calling me a has-been, an old man, and asking me to spend my final autumn as a patriarch reading the adventures of Mondo and the tales of Amadou Koumba to my grandsons, does he know I have no grandsons, does he really know that, and it seems people are all on edge as though I'd done something wrong, and here's Robinette now having her go, it's like some kind of curse, I say tactfully "I don't want to get into a row with you, Robinette, I really care a lot about you, I promise," she says "that's not true, you don't care about me, you don't care about anyone round here, never have, except for the Stubborn Snail," and I retort "why do you think I don't care about you then," "because you're a first-rate liar, it comes as easy as breathing to you, even if you're old and grey you don't care you just go on and on, always lying," I can't find my voice, but still I murmur "I don't think that's true, Robinette," and she carries on regardless "yeah, you're a liar, a real liar," and I feel I can't let that go, so I challenge her "give me an example, tell me when I've lied, and how," and she looks skyward and thinks for a moment and says "have you ever bought me a bottle, just one single little bottle of wine, no, you haven't, not once, you're just a selfish money-grubber, a jerk, you never even looked at me, you loathe me like the plague, that's what it is, have you any idea how many people are after my ass" that completely floors me, I look her straight in the face and I say "help yourself to a bottle, I'll pay for it, this is an important day for me," and to my great surprise she refuses, "no I certainly will not, who do you think I am, a beggar, a poor woman, don't you say that to me, I never asked for anything, you want to get me drunk, then, so you can have your disgusting way with me, is that it, you asshole," and since her voice is really loud, it rises above the general hubbub in the bar and people start to turn round, and I hear the sound of distant laughter, now everyone is watching us, and I feel really embarrassed, I'm going to have to find a way out of this situation, but I can't think of one, and I want to get away from her as fast as possible, I try to see the time on someone's watch, it's Holden's, the tearaway guy who yelled at me a while ago, he's still sitting two tables away and asking the others "can you tell me what happens to the poor little ducks in the cold countries when winter comes, do they put them in zoos, do they migrate to other countries, or do they just get stuck in the snow" and from here I can see his great big watch, hanging round his neck, that's a weird way to wear a watch, it could almost be an alarm clock, maybe that's how Americans wear their watches, those guys must really love everything big, and I manage to make out the time, and I exclaim "my God, it's already nine o'clock in the evening"

I get up to leave the bar "don't you move an inch, Broken Glass, you promised me a bottle, if you move now things are going to get nasty between you and me, you pay for my bottle now," says Robinette, "for fuck's sake, I'm sick of this, make your mind up," I finally start to get mad, "why you getting mad my poppet, it's not good to get mad, it puts lines on your face, you've already got too many of those," says she as I go up to the bar, the Stubborn Snail smiles at me and hands me a bottle of red and whispers in my ear, "so, you going to get it on with Robinette or not," I shake my head and say no, "I think she must be crazy, she's accusing me of all these things, I don't want to leave this bar with things on my conscience, I'm going to buy her this drink she's going on about," and the boss says "no, Broken Glass, you're not going anywhere, you're part of the family, so stop feeling sorry for yourself, go with the girl, she'll take your mind off things, believe me," and he starts sniggering and adds "she wants you, it's as plain as the nose on your face, she really wants you, she's working you over, go on, make an effort, she'll take you to a hotel room or upstairs here, it's fine by me," and I'm not feeling too sure, and I don't really want to get involved with Robinette, I'd rather just forget about her altogether, I'm tired of her unprovoked attacks, my batteries are worn out, I can't imagine getting on top of her, I'm finished with all that, I'm a man who longs for a distant love, so I turn full circle, I want to take a walk along the Avenue of Independence before calling it quits at midnight

*

but just at the moment when I stand up and take a decisive step, I find the Stubborn Snail standing in my path, "where are you off to, my friend," he says, I don't reply, he holds me back by my right hand, asks me what's going on with Robinette, I still say nothing, I hand him the book, he takes it, and straightaway I want to snatch it back, I don't want to give it to him now, I don't know why I take it back, but I try to grab it from him, I can't do it, I beg him to give me my book back, he says "why d'you want your book back now, it's a bit late to write in it now, you hardly ever write in it after ten in the evening, I can tell you want to tear it up, I'm not giving it back, you can have it back tomorrow morning if you want," "give it back now, I want to check something, I promise I'll give it back to you, I don't give a shit about it, I'm not going to tear it up, believe me," the boss flicks quickly through the book and exclaims "but it's nearly full, there are only a few blank pages left, when did you scribble all that then?," and I don't reply, I give a tight smile, the Stubborn Snail comes up close and says quietly "my offer still stands, you go upstairs and sleep in my place, take the keys, you can go up with Robinette if you like, I've spoken to her already, she's up for it," and I push the keys back and manage to get hold of my book, and I have a quick flick through it too, and I say to the Stubborn Snail "go on then, you can keep it now, mission accomplished," and he says in amazement "what d'you mean, mission accomplished, there are still some blank pages left" and he flips through the pages again, concentrating hard this time, before sighing "I didn't look properly the first time, but it's a real mess, this book, there are no full stops, only commas and more commas, sometimes speech marks when someone's talking, that's not right, I think you should tidy it up a bit, don't you, how am I supposed to read all that, if it's all run together like that, you need to leave some spaces, a few breathing places, some pauses, don't you see, I really expected better of you, I'm a bit disappointed, sorry, but your mission isn't accomplished yet, you'll have to start again," and I repeat "mission accomplished," I turn my back on him, and he almost yells "where you off to, Broken Glass?" and I say "I'll be back soon," and I see him leafing through the notebook again, then I hear him reading out loud the first rambling phrases I wrote "*let's say the boss of the bar Credit Gone West gave me this notebook to fill, he's convinced I—Broken Glass—can turn out a book, because one day, for a laugh, I told him about this famous writer who drank like a fish, and had to be picked up off the street when he got drunk, which shows you should never joke with the boss, he takes everything literally*"

I'm struggling to push my way out through the crowd, Mompéro and Dengaki both call out to me, and hold me back, "Broken Glass, come back, come back and take your book," and I pick up my book and my pencil, and I leave the joint, but I write down the dialogue I had earlier with the Stubborn Snail, as though it was happening right now, in the present, and it makes me smile to think that this evening no one knows I'm going to travel with a salmon, and walk along the River Tchinouka, and go and find my mother, and we'll drink, drink once more the waters which carried off the only woman I ever knew who could say "my son, Broken Glass, I love you, and I'll still love you the day you're no more than a piece of rotten garbage," she was my mother, she was the most beautiful woman on earth, and if I had the talent I'd have written a book entitled *The Book of My Mother*, I know someone's already done it, but you can't have too much of a good thing, it would be the unfinished novel, the book of happiness, the book of a man alone, of the first man, the book of wonder, all rolled into one, and on every page I'd write my feelings, my love, my regrets, I'd invent a house on the edge of tears for my mother, some wings too, so she could be queen of the angels in heaven, so she could protect me for ever and ever, and I'd tell her to forgive me for this lousy life, this life and a half that brought me forever into conflict with the red liquid of the Sovinco, and I'd tell her to forgive me for the happiness I never failed to find in inspecting the bottom of my bottles of red, and I know she would forgive me, she'd say "*my son, it's your choice, there's nothing I can do*," and then she'd tell me about my childhood, my long-lost childhood, and how she raised me all by herself, how she fled the village of Louboulou after the death of my father, she'd tell me how I went to the state school in Kouilou, how I made my own way to school, how I walked for two hours, and I would see, as in a mirror, the days of my childhood, running along the beach at the Côte Sauvage, back then I didn't want to grow up, because after twelve years old life is just shit, childhood's our most precious possession, the rest is all just a compilation of blunders and bullshit, let's say that during my youth I looked at each thing with curiosity, I had no fear of the legends that told how in the sea out there lived creatures that were half woman, half fish, which around here we call *mamiwatta*, and, again during these years, the sea stretched out endlessly, while the cormorants came and perched on the beach, their wings grown heavy from wandering, but how many times did I wonder, intrigued, what was unfolding in those fathomless depths, and I believed then that the sea was the sarcophagus of our ancestors, that the salt taste of the water came from their perspiration, and it was this belief that made of me a true child of the Côte, I couldn't stay away from the port for a single day, my mother never said anything, and there was no paternal voice, so I was free to take off, bring back some tuna fish in the evening, which she would dissect, and I'd watch her tear it up into small pieces, which she'd throw, one after the other, into a huge aluminium pot, we'd eat in silence, and in her voice which was both soft and sad, she would say to me "don't go down to the Côte Sauvage, people die down there, there are evil spirits, yesterday they found two children on the beach, their stomachs were bloated, their eyes turned up, I don't want to see you like that one day, if I do I'll follow you, I can't live without you, you're the one thing I've got left to live for," alas, the next day, I'd rise early, cut my lessons, stow away on the Maritime Company truck, a vehicle with worn-out brakes, which took the port employees back to work, they wouldn't throw me off the truck, they were used to kids like me who sometimes helped them with their hard labor, they'd move up a little to make room, so the kids from the Côte could get on, and when I arrived at the port I'd take a good deep breath, I was back in my own world, I saw the gangs of rachitic dogs slavering at the mouth, wanderers too, I'd see their tails curl like springs when they fought over the leftovers of fish with the cormorants and albatrosses, but most of all there were flies, appearing from nowhere, buzzing like bees around a hive, I fixed my eyes on the horizon and wondered how to start the day, whether I'd bring a fish home that evening, though quite often I'd return empty-handed because of the competition from the other children on the Côte, who had muscles bigger than mine, and were used to working on the sea, and some days there were more of us than usual and the fishermen chased us away from their boats, and called us all the names under the seafaring sun, so you had to fight to get hold of just a little fish, you had to be the fastest, and whenever we saw a little boat on the horizon we'd shout for joy, and push each other out of the way and run at last into the water, we had to show the sea workers we had at least touched their nets, that we had helped them bring their boat up on the shore, and we stuck to them like limpets until they rewarded us with fish, but the thing we all dreamed of was bringing a tuna fish home, yes, that was how my childhood was, and I'd see once more the times when I'd read by the light of a storm lantern, the times when my mother would tell me that reading ruined your eyes, and was no use to anyone, reading made you go blind, and I'd carry on reading anyway, and I was permanently hunched over, with sweat on my brow, I discovered the secret of words, I saw right deep inside them, right down to the marrow, I wanted to ruin my eyesight, because to me shortsighted people were intelligent guys, who'd read everything and who were bored by the great uneducated masses, I wanted to read books written in small type, because I was told that these were the books that made you shortsighted, the proof being that the European priests who roamed the Trois-Cents District were all mostly shortsighted and wore large spectacles, and it was probably because they'd read the Jerusalem Bible a thousand and one times, and that's how I grew up, with my eyes glued to the pages of books, till the day when I too would wear a large pair of spectacles like the European priests, till the day when I would tell the entire world, and show them too, that I was an intelligent man, an accomplished man, a man who had read a great deal, and I waited for this day, which never came, and I've never lost sight of it, God knows why, and my sight is probably the one thing about me that's stayed young, it's unjust, it's life, there's nothing I can do, but in a short time I will at last be alone, face-to-face with my mother, in less than two hours now, and we'll talk for a long while, and on the stroke of midnight I will plunge into the depths of these narrow waters, I'll just need to get past the bridge, then I'll be off on my adventure, I'll be happy, because I'll be reunited with my mother, and the next day, there'll be no Broken Glass at Credit Gone West, and for the first time, a broken glass will have been repaired by the good God, and then, at last, from the world beyond, with a smile on my lips, I'll be able to murmur, "mission accomplished"

I must go now, there's nothing left for me to do round here, I must get rid of this book, but then where can I throw it, I don't know, I turn back toward Credit Gone West, though I don't know why, they think I'm crazy because I'm writing even as I push my way through the crowd, and I go past the guy who calls himself Holden, he's still giving me his rebellious adolescent nonsense, asking me "hey, Broken Glass, can you tell me what happens to the poor ducks in cold countries when it's wintertime, do they get put in the zoo or migrate to other countries or do the poor things just get stuck in the snow, I really want to know," he knows it off by heart, he doesn't even change the order of his words each time he asks the question, and I say to him "Holden, don't you think you'd have been better off asking the ducks in the cold countries, while you were still down there, that must be one of the things in that book you're holding, surely," and he looks at me, very disappointed, and murmurs "that's not nice, you don't like ducks, I can tell, I actually really want to know, you just can't imagine how terrible it is for those poor creatures," and he starts sobbing, and I ask him once more what time it is, even if he has got an alarm clock strung round his neck, it's a question of respect, and he refuses to tell me, "I'm not telling you the time if you won't tell me what happens to the poor little ducks in cold countries in wintertime" and then he comes up really close, looks at me for a moment, tells me it's very nearly midnight, so I hand him the book and say to him quietly "my friend, give that to the Stubborn Snail, but you mustn't open it, even if you're in it too, but I decided not to write about your life, I haven't got time, and anyway, I expect you were going to tell me you were a student somewhere abroad, that your friends beat you up in the dorm, that you've been wandering all over Manhattan, you've been in New York, you saw the ducks in winter in Central Park and all that jazz, now don't give me that wide-eyed look, I've never set foot there myself, no one's ever told me your story, Holden, but in a way you almost insulted me, it doesn't matter, you just enjoy your wine, live your life, we'll meet again in the other world, Holden, we'll have a drink together, and you can tell me your entire life story, I'll answer your question, I'll tell you what they do with the poor little ducks in cold countries during wintertime, ciao, old chap, I must be off now, my place is in paradise, and if some cheating angels go telling lies up there to stop me entering by the great wide gate, well, believe me, I'll get in anyway, through the window"